CARTER'S BATTLE

BROTHERHOOD PROTECTORS WORLD

TEAM KOA: BRAVO
BOOK ONE

LORI MATTHEWS

Twisted Page Press LLC

For Suzanne Suarez. So lucky to call you a friend.

ACKNOWLEDGMENTS

First a special thanks to Suzanne Suarez for sharing your story and for giving me the idea for this book. A huge thank you to my editor, Heidi Senesac. You are fantastic. Another amazing individual is my assistant, Sara Mallion. I am so fortunate that I get to work with you.

My fellow writers, Janna MacGregor, Stacey Wilk, Kimberley Ash and Tiara Inserto, you are all truly amazing authors but even more, you're the friends that keep me grounded. Thank you ladies for always being there.

My super supportive family also deserves a big thanks. They keep me laughing and make every day better.

And last but not least, to you the reader. You are the reason I write. Thanks for the love.

BROTHERHOOD PROTECTORS
ORIGINAL SERIES BY ELLE JAMES

Brotherhood Protectors Hawaii World
Team Koa Bravo
Bowie's Battle - Jen Talty
Carter's Battle - Lori Matthews
Flint's Battle - Kris Norris
Quinn's Battle - Regan Black

Brotherhood Protectors Hawaii World
Team Koa Alpha
Lane Unleashed - Regan Black
Harlan Unleashed - Stacey Wilk
Raider Unleashed - Lori Matthews
Waylen Unleashed - Jen Talty
Kian Unleashed - Kris Norris

CARTER'S BATTLE

BROTHERHOOD PROTECTORS WORLD

TEAM KOA: BRAVO
BOOK ONE

LORI MATTHEWS

CHAPTER 1

CARTER NOLAN LEANED back in his chair and took a gulp of his ice-cold beer. It had been a long day and the beer tasted refreshing going down his parched throat. He and his SEAL teammates had spent the day testing radio equipment out at the Brotherhood Protectors ranch on the big island of Hawai'i. *A fucking colossal waste of time.* He hissed out a long sigh.

"What's up with you?" Bowie Colson demanded. "The beer not cold enough?"

Carter frowned at his teammate. "Just a long day and a big bootless errand. We're testing equipment we know works. It's just bullshit."

"Well, it's the kind of bullshit I like," Flint O'Connell grunted. "Four weeks on the Big

Island? Dude, Hawai'i is a fucking vacation, and you should be happier about it. Look at this place. When was the last time we had a chance to chill that wasn't in a dive bar in some godforsaken corner of the earth?"

Carter glanced around Ohana's. He still couldn't believe Waylen Brown and the rest of his team owned the bar. They all claimed it was the best place around, and from what Carter could see, they weren't wrong. Surfboards and tiki masks hung on the walls. The long wooden bar gleamed in the setting sun. The jukebox in the corner played Margaritaville, and Jimmy Buffet had just stepped on a pop-top. Not many better places to waste away. Or waste time.

Flint was right. This was so much better than the places where they usually had downtime.

He turned over his cell and glanced at the screen. Still nothing. He returned the device to the face-down position again. Castle said he'd text when he knew something. Carter swigged more beer and tried to relax.

Quinn Kennedy pointed at the phone. "You're like a teenage girl waiting for some guy to text her. The CO said he'd text when he knew something. It's only been twenty-four hours. Give the man a chance. It can't be easy to conduct this kind of investigation without tipping his hand."

"I know," Carter agreed. "But I just don't like this shit hanging over our heads. McCarthy and the rest of those assholes are really fucking slick, and it makes me sick to know they're wreaking havoc, but we can't prove it."

Quinn nodded. "We're all pissed about the situation, but Castle said to come here and put up a pretext like we believe these last few missions have been plagued by equipment failure. We're here to test it. We gotta do what the CO says. Have a little faith, brother."

Carter bit his tongue. He knew Quinn was right. Letting it go was damn hard because now it was personal. He lacked patience most days, but he was majorly pissed that four men on their team were crooked and were out to get him and his friends killed.

"Can I get you boys another round?" the bartender called from across the room. It was late afternoon and more customers were trickling in.

"Lighten up. The view here is excellent." Quinn kicked Carter's chair as he gave the cute bartender a nod and a big smile.

Carter was pretty sure Quinn wasn't talking about the exterior view on the other side of the bar. The squawk of electronic interference filled the bar and people groaned.

"Sorry, sorry," called a pretty woman from the small stage at the back of the bar.

"Hey, Moana, you singing tonight?" asked the bartender who was setting snacks out on the bar.

"Yeah, Dahlia. Thought I'd do a set."

"Awesome. So glad you're back."

A dark-haired woman brought another round of beers to their table. The way she moved and kept her eye on the bar made Carter think she might have been some kind of law enforcement in a past life.

"Can I get you guys anything else?"

"I think we're good, Ms…" Flint let his voice peter out.

"Emery."

"Nice to meet you, Ms. Emery. I'm Flint."

"No it's just Emery." She gave him a nod and then turned on her heel and headed back toward the bar.

Bowie snorted. "I think she's blown away by your charm, Flint. She practically had to run across the bar to stop herself from crawling into your lap."

"I'm glad to see you understand the situation." Flint's grin was broad.

Carter let his friends' banter wash over him as he practiced patterned breathing to quiet his mind. He needed a distraction if he was going to get through these next four weeks. Something to keep his mind busy and stop the review of their last few missions that seemed to play on a vicious loop in his brain.

A petite, dark-haired woman carrying a satchel emerged from the back office. Her long black hair was contained in a ponytail that swished just above her curvy butt as she walked. She glanced at the stage and then turned to the bartender. "Emery, is Moana singing tonight?"

"Yeah. I'm super-stoked. It's been ages since she's performed here. You gonna stay?" Emery sat down on a stool at the bar. "Stay, Mia. It'll be fun."

The curvy woman shook her head ruefully. "I'd love to. I haven't heard Moana sing in a long time and it would be great to hang with you guys, but I have to go home and fix my plumbing."

The bartender smirked. "Is that a euphemism?"

Carter smiled. He'd been thinking the same

thing. Now, this was the type of distraction he needed. The beautiful woman with the sexy smile was exactly the kind of woman he'd like occupy his time.

"I wish," Mia snorted. Then she let out a big sigh. "Sadly, it's the truth. I don't know why I thought buying a house was a good idea. My shower went kablooey this morning so now I have to go home and see what the hell is wrong with it."

"Your shower can wait," Emery cajoled.

Mia bit her lip and Carter took notice. *Yeah, stay, Mia.* He willed the mental instruction to her from across the room.

"Sorry, can't tonight. But we'll do it soon. Promise." She waved to her friends and then moved toward the exit. She glanced in their direction and her gaze locked with Carter's.

He knew two things instantly. One, she was even sexier than he thought with dark haunting eyes, and two, she was worried about something.

The woman disappeared through the doorway of the bar. A vague sense of unease crept up Carter's spine. With his thumbnail, he scraped at the label on his beer bottle as he tried to shake the feeling, but he knew trying to dispel the sensation was useless. He'd been feeling this way for a while now and somehow that woman, Mia, had just kicked the feeling into overdrive.

He glanced around the table at his friends. To him, it felt like there was a storm coming and they were all out of shelter.

CHAPTER 2

MIA RYAN STARED at the screen in front of her. The numbers didn't make sense. Thinking maybe she was just tired and not seeing things correctly, she rubbed her eyes, to no avail. Half the previous night had been spent tinkering with her shower before finally getting it to work but she'd soaked herself in the process. She was running on little sleep and limited food. The three stops before this one, the last one on her docket for today, had all turned up accounting issues that she'd had to take extra time to solve so she'd been late coming to Lono's Coffee House.

Mia opened her eyes again and stared at the screen. Nothing had changed. The numbers on the spreadsheet remained the same, goading her into questioning her own sanity. There was no way the line items could be this far off the mark. It had to be a typo somewhere or maybe even a lot of typos. Errors she knew she hadn't made.

Scrolling back to the top of the sheet, Mia started down the columns of numbers one more time. She'd already double-checked the figures once, but she was willing to give it another try. Maybe she was just seeing things. Never hurts to triple-check things. And wasn't that the definition of insanity? Doing something again and again and hoping for a different outcome?

Ten minutes later, her heart hammered against her ribcage. Mia leaned back in the chair and stared open-mouthed at the screen. She wasn't wrong. The numbers weren't wrong. Lono's Coffee House was broke. More than broke. With these numbers, it was going under. But how could they be so different from last month? Numbers were her jam, and there was no scenario in which she could have been this far off.

Mia clicked on the screen and brought up last month's spreadsheet. Staring at the screen, her mouth dropped open again as all the air left her lungs. "No…" these were not the numbers from last month. They couldn't be. She'd balanced the books last month and Lono's had made a healthy profit. Where had that almost ten percent growth gone? These numbers said the coffee house was...bankrupt. There wasn't enough money in the accounts to pay the baristas salaries.

She frantically clicked back for several months. All these numbers were wrong. An unnerving queasiness rose in her stomach. No, not wrong. The numbers were right. But they were different to what she'd been shown. A thought suddenly dawned; this was a different set, a second set, of books. Akela, the owner of Lono's was cooking the books. Mia's stomach churned. She wanted to puke. Hiding the real numbers on these spread sheets while showing Mia something else entirely. But why bother? Obviously, she had someone doing her real books so why hire Mia at all?

Mia's head spun. Akela was using Mia to legitimize the business. Mia had a good rep as the island's go-to accountant for small businesses. Businesses sought her out to do their books. If Mia was working on the accounts then they couldn't be falsified. Mia, as Akela's accountant, helped keep up the front that the client wasn't doing anything shady.

She stared at the screen as she contemplated her friendship with Akela Kahue. They'd come up together in the surfing world. Both had turned pro the same year, but then Mia blew out her knee. Akela had gone on to win some competitions. They hadn't run into each other again until a couple of years ago, but the bonds formed during their teen years were strong. Especially since Mia had lost her parents.

Stunned, Mia just couldn't accept this. Why would Akela do this? It certainly explained why she'd been so jumpy and out of sorts for the last while.

A bang against the shared wall with the front end of the shop brought her back to her current situation with a thump. The queasy sensation hadn't eased, and now she broke out in a sweat. Mia wasn't even supposed to be here at this moment. Thanks to all the other stuff she'd come across in her other clients' books, she was running late. She should've been at Lono's Coffee House a couple of hours ago. Instead, she'd walked in late and come right back to the office by herself. The computer was already up and running and didn't require a password, so Mia had just opened the file. Or, rather, what she thought was the file. She glanced now at the name and realized it was slightly different from the file she usually worked on. "Son of a bitch," she mumbled.

Clicking the other file, her usual spreadsheet opened in front of her. Okay, these were the numbers she was used to working with. She bit her lip. This was a huge problem. That would teach her to worry about her plumbing. Now leaky pipes seemed like the least of her worries.

Another thump made Mia jump. "Shit," she mumbled as she quickly went through the fake spreadsheet. She wasn't ready to confront her friend just yet, if ever. The repercussions could be severe, even to the extent of jeopardizing Mia's reputation. She needed time to play the whole thing out in her mind. Pulling a thumb drive out of her bag, she quickly stuck it in the computer and copied the alternate files. Were these the real numbers? Shaking her head, she dropped the small drive into her pocket and closed the file just as the door to the office burst open.

"Mia!" Akela Kahue stared at her friend in surprise. "When did you get here?" Her gaze quickly lit on the computer and then back to Mia.

That was all the confirmation she needed.

The panic in her friend's eyes make Mia's stomach drop. She'd known Akela for way too many years not to recognize the look for what it was.

Guilt.

Deflect and deny were the two words at the top of her head. "A little bit ago. You weren't around so I just came back here and got to work." Mia gathered her things. "I'm finished, actually," she said, standing up. "Everything looks great." She prayed that the hollow feeling roiling her stomach wasn't written across her face. "Any big plans for the weekend?" Anything to distract from the situation.

Akela glanced at the computer once again and frowned. "This weekend? No. No big plans. My little brother has football practice, so I need to take him to that."

"How is Kai doing? Is his knee on the mend?" Mia came out from around the desk and started toward the door.

"He's doing much better. The surgery was a success and he's excited to be back on the field." Akela's eyes narrowed slightly, and Mia knew she was being watched closely for any sign that she had a clue about what was going on. Her grip on her bag slipped a bit, thanks to her sweaty palms.

"What about you?" Akela asked. "Any big plans?"

Mia snorted. "I spent last night fixing my shower. Tonight, I have a date with my washing machine, and I will probably spend all day tomorrow catching up on chores. I'm hoping to get over to Ohana's and hang with the girls at some point, but I'll have to see how it goes. You should join us."

Akela gave a small nod. "That sounds like fun. I heard Moana is back in town."

"Yes," Mia said in an overly bright voice. "She was singing at Ohana's last night, but I had to miss it." She gave a small shrug. "The whole shower thing. Oh, the joys of home ownership, right?" She needed to get out of there before Akela got suspicious. "Anyway, gotta go. You know what Friday night traffic is like. I want to stop and pick up a pizza on the way home. I'll text you if we get together at Ohana's. Otherwise, I'll see you next month." She offered Akela a smile and brushed past the other woman.

"Yeah, see you."

"Good luck to your brother this season," Mia called as she left the office and walked rapidly toward the shop's front door. Her heartbeat pulsed in her ears, and her palms were slick with sweat. She hit the door and was across the parking lot like a shot. Five minutes later she was steering out of the lot and heading home. Mia decided to order pizza once she got there and have it delivered. She didn't think her knees would hold her any longer.

Thirty minutes later, she pulled into her driveway, turned off her car, and rested her head on the steering wheel, breathing steadily and trying to control her rapid pulse.

What the hell was she going to do? She didn't want to cause trouble for Akela, but she wanted no part in whatever mess the other woman was wrapped up in.

She cast about in her mind for solutions but came up with nothing. Emery was working this weekend at Ohana's. Should she ask her some hypothetical questions? As a cop, Emery would know how much trouble Mia might be in. But on the other hand, if she asked then she would be dragging another friend into this mess, and she didn't want to do that. Besides, Emery would probably go arrest Akela. She was kind of a stickler as far as rules went, a trait Mia had always admired.

Mia hauled her butt out of the car and made her way inside her little house. She closed the door and leaned her back against it. The house was small and needed tons of repairs, but it always made Mia feel so proud when she walked through the door. This house was hers. Hers. Nothing brought her more joy.

She set her bag on the floor by the side table as she looked around the main living space. She'd decorated in a beachy vibe, so the furniture was white with throw pillows of varying shades of blue. The floor was a light wood and so were the coffee table and matching end tables. The space was a small but comfortable and it smelled like the flowers she'd cut this morning from the tiny back garden.

After changing her dress slacks and brightly colored gauzy blouse that made up her typical work attire for a pair of board shorts and a tank top, she went back out to the kitchen and placed an order for a veggie pizza. She had a craving for a large glass of wine and grabbed the stemless goblet to pour herself a generous serving. Hooking her foot around the leg of a stool, she hauled it away from the island that separated the kitchen from the living room. Letting out a long breath, she dropped onto the cushioned seat and took a sip of crisp cool wine. *That was much better.*

She tried to relax but her mind kept going back to what was on the thumb drive. How long had all this been going on? Was Akela okay? Why the hell would she get involved in this type of thing? She was a straight shooter, or at least she had been during their surfing days.

"Shit," Mia mumbled as she went to her bag and retrieved the thumb drive. She unplugged her laptop and picked it up from the coffee table and then set it down again on the island. She resituated herself on the stool and opened the screen. No answers would come until she knew more details. Mia knew it was stupid to keep looking at the information, but she just couldn't help herself. Curiosity was killing her.

Pulling up the files, Mia took a bracing sip of her wine and then dove in. She went back month by month to see where everything went wrong. Ten months ago. Lono's Coffee was making money, and then eight months ago, something happened. Her friend had started taking out massive amounts of cash, way more than was coming in. "Why in the hell would you do that, Akela?" Mia murmured.

A knock at the door made her jump. Pizza.

"About time." She was starving. Closing her laptop, she hopped off the stool, went over to the door, and opened it. Akela stood on her front step.

"Oh…I was expecting a pizza delivery. What are you doing here?" Mia tried not to panic. *Be calm*. This was her friend. She'd known Akela since they were teenagers. *No need to worry.*

"You saw it didn't you?" Akela demanded.

"What are you talking about?"

"Don't play innocent with me. I know you saw it."

Mia frowned. "Akela, I…" she stopped speaking as the pizza delivery guy pulled into her driveway. "Why don't you come in? Do you want some pizza?" Not that she wanted Akela to come into her home, her refuge, but what choice did she have?

Akela came in and moved out of the way. Mia dealt with the pizza guy and then went to the kitchen and got down a couple of plates.

"I don't want pizza. I want the truth," Akela demanded.

Mia set a slice of warm gooey cheese pizza on one plate. She tried to remain calm, but suddenly, she found herself angry. Exhaustion crept up on her and although she knew she should keep her mouth shut, she just didn't have the patience any longer to deal with this bullshit, friendship aside.

She met Akela's gaze. "Yeah, I saw it. You're cooking your books and using me to make them look good. Thanks for that," Mia snarled.

Akela pointed at her. "You shouldn't have been poking around where you don't belong."

"Bullshit. You hired me to do your books. That's what I did. Not my fault you're crooked. You named the spreadsheet almost the same damn name. How was I supposed to know? You can't blame any of this shit on me. This is all you, right down to the fake receipts and invoices you provided."

All the color drained from Akela's face and she burst into tears.

Mia stared. "Shit." She plopped her plate on the counter, and then went and hugged her friend. "It's okay," she muttered.

This situation was a lot of things but okay wasn't one of them. She had no idea how to help her friend fix this, but Mia knew it wasn't going to be easy.

Akela stepped back and wiped her eyes with the back of her hand. Mia reached over and grabbed a paper towel, then handed it to her.

"Here. Sit and tell me what happened. How did you get into this mess?"

Akela sat on a stool and Mia took the one beside her. She reached for her plate and then took a bite of pizza while she waited for the other woman to stop sniffling. No point in not eating while it was hot. Mostly, she thought it was a good idea to have her mouth full so she didn't yell at Akela for being fucking stupid and falsifying her business records. God, was this a felony or a misdemeanor? Didn't matter. There was never a legitimate reason to create two sets of records. But Mia figured Akela must think she had a good reason.

"I know what you're thinking." Akela gave her a rueful smile. "I would be thinking it, too, if I were you. How could I do something so stupid?"

Mia tried to keep her face neutral, but she could tell by the look on Akela's face that she wasn't so successful. She bit off another large mouthful of her slice.

"Yeah, well it didn't start off like this." She played with the paper towel. "Kai needed surgery. The café was doing okay. You know what I mean. Doing okay enough to support us but not doing well enough to do anything crazy. Kai's surgery was insanely expensive, but the doctor said it was necessary. I scraped together all I had but it wasn't going to be enough, not to mention Kai and I needed to eat." She let out a long sigh. "Bobby Kamaka came to see me."

Mia froze. That was a name she never wanted to hear again. Her heart rate escalated, making it hard to draw a full breath. The pizza solidified into a rock in her gut. She tried to swallow the bite she had in her mouth, but it had turned to sawdust. She set the slice down, trying not to choke. This situation called for a healthy dose of liquid courage. Hopping off the stool, she hurried to the fridge, pulled out a bottle of wine, then a second glass, filled it generously, then refilled her own. She came back around the counter and sat down handing one to Akela.

"So, you know him then," the other woman said as she studied Mia over the rim of her glass and then took a large gulp of her wine.

"Yeah," Mia croaked out and then followed suit. "You tell me yours and I'll tell you mine."

Akela nodded. "Bobby follows high school sports, and he knew Kai had…has talent. He also knew we weren't in the best financial shape. He said if I let him use my basement at the store to host a few poker games, then he'd help me out with the surgery."

Mia closed her eyes. She knew where this was going. "Fucking Bobby Kamaka is a pimple on the butt of a donkey."

"Yup" Akela agreed. She rubbed her face. "It seemed like a small thing and I really needed the money. Kai...Kai was devastated about his knee. He'd always thought he would make the NFL. His dreams were shattered and I...I just didn't have the heart to tell him that we'd have to wait about the surgery, that his season was over. Since our mom left, there's only the two of us. I couldn't be the one who killed his dream. He worked so hard for it."

"So you said yes." Mia sighed. Saying yes to Bobby was akin to opening the door to the devil.

"At first, it was just as he'd said. He held games in my basement a couple times a week, and he paid me a fee. By the time the surgery came around, I had enough to cover it." Akela took another gulp of wine. "Kai came through with flying colors, which was great, but what I hadn't counted on was the physical therapy he'd need to get back on the field. I mean, I knew he'd need therapy, but in order to play football again, he'd need twice as much. I...I just didn't have the money and had no way to get it. I'd already begged, borrowed, or stolen everything I could."

Mia's stomach rolled. "What did Bobby do?"

Akela slumped in her chair. "He held more games in the basement. Then he wanted me to cater other games for him. He paid me double for the catering and gave me extra for the games, but it still wasn't enough and I started getting nervous. Bobby kept coming into the café demanding I do more catering or close early so he could host a longer game. I finally told him no more. I wasn't doing anything else. I wanted him gone. Kai was just going to have to take the extra time to get back on the field."

Mia didn't want to ask. Knowing Bobby and how he was, the answer was going to be rough. Finally, she said in a quiet voice, "What did he do?"

Akela started crying again. "He grabbed Kai and had two goons bring him to the café after it closed. She choked back a sob. "One of the guys held a baseball bat to Kai's knee and Bobby said if I didn't do exactly as he wanted, he would smash Kai's other knee so he could never play football again and then he grabbed me, and said he might not stop there."

"He threatened to rape you?"

She shrugged but wiped her face on the paper towel. "Not in so many words but his meaning was clear." She chugged more of her wine. "He claimed he had people working in the police department, so if I reported him he'd know. Then he threatened to hurt Emery. He knew that I knew her, and he said if I went to her, he'd make sure to take her out."

Mia reached over and hugged the other woman. "Oh, Akela, I am so, so sorry." This was awful. Worse than awful. This was hell and there was no way out. Mia straightened. "I can guess the rest. That's when he started to run the gambling money through the café's books."

Akela nodded. "He ran off a lot of my regulars by just hanging out. Everyone knows he's bad news. No one wants to be around him." She let out a shuddering breath. "Mia, he said he'd take me down with him if I did anything to put him in jail. I had supplied my place to be used for gambling, which is illegal in Hawaii, and now he's cooking my books or, his accountant is."

Mia didn't think it was possible, but she felt worse. "Who is the accountant?" she asked dread filling every cell of her being.

"Donny Nakamura"

"Oh my God." Mia thought for a moment she might actually be ill. The room swam. She took a deep breath and held it for a minute until everything righted itself and then she let it out.

Akela stared at her. "Your turn. How do you know Bobby and Donny?"

Opening her mouth was straight-up difficult. The whole nightmare had been in her rearview mirror for two years now and talking about it was going to bring it all back into focus, as if it had actually ever truly receded. Akela's situation had brought the horror all the way back again and landed on her chest with both damn feet. She hated Bobby Kamaka and Donny Nakamura with a fierceness that scared her.

"I am pretty sure they killed my parents."

CHAPTER 3

CARTER LEANED against the side of the Jeep and studied the ocean. Hawaii was much more than he'd bargained for. Sure, it had beaches, but it also had pastureland and jagged black volcanic rock. Rain forests were dominant on one end, while the other side resembled a desert. It amazed him how different the Big Island could be around every curve in the road.

He sipped his water as he gazed at a surfer paddling furiously. The incoming wave was a big one and the guy managed to catch it just right. He was good and made it look easy which it most definitely was not. Carter had tried it a few times but could never really master the skill. Now that he was going to be here for a while maybe it was time to really learn.

A group of women in bikinis strolled by. Maybe he could learn from one of the many gorgeous women that seemed to live on this island. That would make all of the inevitable falls less painful. His brain flicked to the woman from the bar, Mia. He wouldn't mind having her teach him. Seeing her in a bikini would go a long way to curing any hurt that surfing might inflict.

He glanced at his watch. It wasn't like Castle to be late. Especially not this late. A knot of worry that had been building since Castle had told them they were going to Hawai'i got a little bigger. *Damn.* He hated all this. Hated suspecting that the other four members of the new team were dirty. Hated the fact that he and his best friends had been left hanging too many times for it to be coincidence, and hated the fact that he was pretty sure the other four team members, McCarthy, Hendrick, Jones, and Ferrero, had killed the men he and his teammates were brought in to replace.

His cell sounded and he answered before the first ring had finished. "Sir."

"Nolan." Castle's voice was weary. "How's Hawai'i?"

"Good, sir. The weather is awesome, the views are incredible, and the beer is ice cold."

Castle snorted. "Does that mean you're not getting any work done? I sent you there to run diagnostics on the radio system and other equipment on purpose."

Carter replied. "We're doing it, sir, although we both know it's not the equipment. But we're trying to enjoy the environment as well. No point in not doing it."

"Fine. Just don't enjoy it too much," Castle warned. "If I get any calls about you guys misbehaving, it's not going to help things on this end."

"And how are things going on that end, sir?" Carter couldn't stop himself from asking. There was a long pause and Carter's gut tightened.

"It's going. To be honest, Nolan, I'm not finding much. I've been over what happened to the former members of the team, and it was a shit show. But there's nothing I can point to that says it was on purpose. My men were cut off from the others and got taken out by sniper fire. I can't prove anything else."

It was Carter's turn to be silent. "Do you believe us, sir?" He didn't want to ask because it made him feel like a stupid kid looking for reassurance, but he needed his CO to believe in him and his teammates...believe that they weren't imagining things. Believe that four members of their own team were trying to kill them.

"I do, son. I might not have been able to find anything out of line about the others dying just yet, but I have managed to uncover a money trail. It's small but it might lead to bigger. That's all I'm going to tell you for now. You and the others need to be patient and run the diagnostics. I know the situation isn't ideal, but this is how we have to handle this investigation. As soon as I have something solid, I'll get back to you. Until then, test the equipment and stay out of trouble." Castle hung up.

Carter sighed and slipped his phone back in his pocket as the surfer tried to catch another wave. This one broke oddly and the surfer got swept off his board and pulled under the waves. Carter knew just how he felt. He and his teammates had been broadsided by the unexpected. They were all trying to cope in their way, but it was damn hard. They were men of action. Sitting around and waiting for Castle to complete some kind of clandestine investigation sat like an over-weighted dive suit.

Lately, lots of things seemed to fall outside his three-foot world, the area that, as a SEAL, he could control. He'd put in his twenty years, and re-enlistment papers were in his near future. Carter never imagined he'd be the one to pull the plug. In his mind, the Navy would have to push him out the door. Or carry him out in a simple pine box. Recently, however, the signs pointed the way to knowing it might be time to go.

He wouldn't leave his brothers, though. If they all re-upped, then he would as well. It was something they'd all have to discuss.

The surfer caught another big wave and rode it all the way to the shore. There was something about Hawai'i. Something that made it seem like he had a future outside of the military. Something that appealed to him in a big way.

His phone went off again and he pulled it out, glancing at the screen as he answered. "Quinn, what's up?"

"We're gonna meet at Ohana's. You in?"

"Sure. What else do I have to do on a Friday night?" Carter straightened and then got into the Jeep.

"Okay. I'm on my way to grab a shower and then I'm gonna head over. See you there in about an hour or so."

"Sounds good." Carter clicked off the call and glanced at the setting sun. The surfer was walking across the sand, heading towards the parked cars. It was time for everyone to leave this beach. The dread lining his gut blossomed uncomfortably, and Carter just couldn't shake it. If Castle didn't find anything then they were going to have to go back out on missions with four assholes whom they all suspected. An unhappy occurrence that was way beyond *not good*. Every mission was dangerous, but this FUBAR situation was truly fucked up beyond all reasoning. It fell under the *dangerous as hell* category. Being distracted by worrying about their own guys killing them was deadly. Hard to catch the enemy when you were worried about dying from friendly fire.

He let out a long breath and started the Jeep. He'd have to tell the others there was no news yet, which sucked balls, but there wasn't much he could do. His CO was working behind the scenes to prove what Carter knew in his gut. The team had dirty members; assholes who could get them killed. But he was in Hawai'i, and there was not one thing he could do to help at the moment. He needed to let it go or he would be tied up in knots.

He rolled his shoulders to release the tense tangles giving him a headache, then pulled out of the parking lot and away from the beach. Maybe

Mia would be at the bar tonight. He was determined to chat with her. Maybe get her to teach him to surf. The thought of her in a bikini made him almost forget the shitty situation and kept him smiling the whole way across the island to the bar.

CHAPTER 4

"Look Akela, I don't really want to get into the details," Mia hedged.

The other woman frowned. "You said you'd tell me your story if I told you mine. Are you saying you lied to me?"

Mia gritted her teeth. "Who is the liar here? You are the one with cooked books. You're the one using me as cover to hide what you're doing."

She held up her hands in surrender. "You're right. I'm sorry. I'm so sorry I ever involved you in this mess." Akela rubbed her face with her hands.

Mia let out a long breath and took the plunge. This story still shook her and spewing it out fast was the only way to live through the retelling.

"Long story short, I used to gamble. Bobby made money off me. When I decided to stop, Bobby and his money man, Donny, didn't like it. They threatened to hurt my family but then Bobby went to jail. Someone ratted out his gambling business, and they found drugs in one of his places, which made it much more serious." She'd been so relieved when Bobby had gone to jail. She felt like she could breathe again. Until...

"Two years ago, just after Bobby got out, my parents died in a weird car accident no one could reasonably explain. The evidence suggested that some animal must have run across the road and they swerved to avoid it."

"But why would Bobby want to hurt your family, your parents?"

"Because he was making serious money off of me. He staked me and I was good. When I stopped, he lost his cash cow, and he wasn't happy about it. Then he got arrested just after he threatened them. Two weeks after he got out of jail... they were dead."

Akela's mouth formed a perfect O. She blinked. "That does not make me feel better."

Mia shrugged. "No, I guess it doesn't. I'm sorry but you should know Bobby and Donny will do exactly what they threaten to do unless we find a way to stop it."

"We?" Akela raised an eyebrow. "Are you going to help me?"

Mia bit her lip. "I'm not going to do your books anymore for sure, but I don't want you or your brother to get hurt either. And to be clear, I would love to see Bobby and Donny get what they deserve." She took a sip of her wine and then set the glass down on the counter. "Let me think on it. Maybe there's something I can do or some kind of plan we can make to get you out of this jam." She hurried on after Akela's look turned hopeful. "I'm not promising anything, but I'll do some thinking about it, okay?"

Akela nodded. "That's fair. Bobby is going to get suspicious when you quit though."

Mia shrugged. "I can't risk my reputation. It's taken me too long to build my client list. If I get exposed as cooking someone's books, even if I didn't do it, I'll lose my livelihood. I'm sorry, Akela, I just can't risk that."

"I know, I shouldn't have said anything. I'm so sorry I got you involved. I just ...I'm just trapped.."

Mia stood. "Like I said, I'll think on it a bit and see what I can come up with. Since I was at the café today, we have another month before Bobby and Donny will find out I'm not doing the books anymore. By then we'll have a good story lined up. I'm chasing some bigger clients at the moment. If some of them come through, I'd have to quit doing your books anyway. Your job just doesn't pay enough."

Akela got up off the stool as well. "Okay, that sounds reasonable." She leaned in and gave Mia a quick hug. "Thanks for listening. I feel better now that someone knows my secret. Even if we can't come up with something, somehow, I don't feel so alone."

Mia nodded as she walked to the door. "I'm glad you feel better."

They hugged again briefly and then Akela left. Mia watched her go and then closed the door and locked it. She wanted to run around and make sure the entire house was locked down. Bobby Kamaka scared the crap out of her. She hated him with every fiber of her being. She was dead certain he'd killed her parents, which made a huge part of her want nothing to do with him.

But…

But the part of her that had gotten involved with him in the first place, that darker part of her soul, that part wanted revenge and wanted it so badly it was a sour taste in her mouth. There had to be a way to take down Bobby and Donny. She just needed to figure it out.

Glancing at her watch, she quickly decided that Ohana's might just be the place to start. If Emery was there, she could pose some hypothetical questions and maybe get some answers. She wouldn't involve her friend just yet. She didn't have any concrete evidence to bring to her. Akela was the only one who was on the hook at the moment and there was no way she wanted her friend to go to jail, even if their relationship had cooled over the years. Akela had worked too hard and long to let Bobby Kamaka bring her down. She and Kai deserved some happiness and deserved to be safe from assholes.

MIA CHANGED into a black tank top and a pair of faded jeans. She jammed her feet into her favorite cowboy boots and ran a brush through her long black hair before heading out the door. She didn't want to think too much about the mess with Akela or Bobby, or she might lose her nerve. To quiet her racing thoughts, she turned the music up high and sang at the top of her lungs as she drove. She'd never sing on stage because she was god-awful, but in the shower and in the car, it was okay to let loose.

Twenty minutes later, she walked into Ohana's and slid onto a barstool.

"Hey, Mia," Dahlia called from the other side of the bar.

"Hey, girl. How's it going? How was Moana last night?"

Dahlia sauntered over to stand in front of Mia. "Amazing. That girl has gotten better since she left."

"Sorry I missed it."

"Did you get your shower fixed?" Dahlia asked as she held up a wine glass.

Mia shook her head. "Tonic water. I had a glass already and I have to be able to drive. Yes, I took care of the issue with my shower, but the list of things that need to be repaired just gets longer, I swear." She glanced around the bar. A good crowd was building. The place would be jam-packed before long. "Is Emery around?"

Dahlia shook her head. "Not yet. She'll be by in a bit. She's just getting off duty."

Mia sat at the bar and watched Dahlia work. People came in twos and threes, and it was getting hard to have any kind of conversation without yelling. Mia glanced at her watch. Maybe it was time to pack it in. She'd text Emery tomorrow and see if they could have a chat.

"Excuse me, but is this seat taken?" a deep voice said in her right ear.

She turned and her gaze was captured by a set of the bluest eyes she'd ever seen. It was the guy from yesterday. She'd noticed his eyes from across the bar, but up close they were mesmerizing, sexy as sin. "Uh…no. It's free."

He sat down beside her and immediately turned to face her. "Can I buy you a drink?"

She blinked. "No thanks. I'm just on my way out."

Those blue eyes studied her. "You look worried. What are you worried about?"

Mia frowned. "Sorry?"

"You look worried. I asked what you're so worried about?"

"Look, Mr…?" She lifted a hand in question.

"Carter Nolan." Blue Eyes offered his hand.

She slipped hers into his and it disappeared completely. The guy was huge. Much bigger than she was. And sexy as hell. There was something about the curve of his lips that made all kinds of oh-so-bad but really wonderful thoughts flipping through her head.

She tugged her hand free and stood. "I've gotta go."

"Teach me to surf," Carter said.

"What?"

"Teach me to surf. I hear you're an amazing surfer. I need to learn."

Mia stared. What was this guy's problem? She needed to go. This day was weird enough as it was and now it seemed to be headed further into uncharted territory. "I—"

He leaned in and spoke quietly, his breath tickling her ear. "If you won't tell me what's worrying you, then at least teach me to surf. Everyone says it's a great way to relax and be Zen. I need a little Zen in my life."

Mia opened her mouth to decline but found herself nodding instead. "It is a good way to be Zen." She met his gaze. Bobby Kamaka was trouble. If she really was going to get further involved in this mess, then maybe she could take a bit of time and go surfing first.

"Fine," she said. "Give me your phone." She put her digits into his phone and put his in her own. "I'll text you where and when." With that she gave Dahlia a wave and pushed away from the bar. She was afraid if she didn't leave right then, she'd regret her decision and she really didn't want to do that. Sexy as all get out Carter Nolan was just the distraction she needed.

Mia walked toward her car just as the band started playing. The sounds of country music followed her out to the parking lot. Maybe teaching Blue Eyes to surf wasn't the best idea but it gave her something to look forward to. She glanced up at the moon. It was almost full. Might be nice to get out on the waves again. It had been a while.

She dug in her purse for her keys as someone grabbed her arm. Mia swung around to see Bobby standing there, with one of his henchmen on either side of her. "Son of a bitch."

"It's nice to see you too, Mia. It's been a while."

"What the fuck do you want?" She tried to sound tough, unbothered, but her heart bumped against her rib cage and her mouth had gone dry. Should she scream? Would anyone hear her over the band? She glanced around trying not to look as frantic as she felt.

"Careful, Mia. Don't push me," Bobby growled.

"What do you want?" she demanded again.

Bobby's cold smile in the bright moonlight made her skin crawl. "I think you and I need to chat."

Mia shook her head. Whatever she'd been thinking when Akela had been at her place was wrong. She'd allowed time and her need for vengeance to cloud her judgment. Getting involved with Bobby was a huge mistake. She'd managed to get out alive last time, but her parents hadn't been so lucky. She wasn't about to risk her life for Akela or Kai. *Sorry, no way.*

"I ran into Akela at her house. You were at the café today. I was told you went back to the office by yourself and left in a hurry. You know what's going on."

Mia shook her head. "I don't know what—"

"Save the bullshit. Akela told me the truth."

Fuck. Akela had sold her out. Probably didn't have a choice. Still now what the hell was she going to do? Her instinct was to scream and run.

"What do you want, Bobby?" Mia took a small step backward. Maybe if she could get a head start, she could make it back to the bar and get help.

Bobby gestured with his chin and his two henchmen, Tweedle Dee and Tweedle Dumb, each grabbed an arm. "I think we need to talk about what you know and about how you're going to help me."

"I'm not helping you," Mia declared defiantly.

"I wouldn't be too sure," Bobby grinned coldly. "Put her in the van."

Mia tugged against the two bruisers, but it was no use. She wasn't getting away. Glancing desperately around the parking lot, her eyes fell on the door to the bar. Was someone there in the shadows? She opened her mouth to yell for help when they threw her in the back of a white van, her scream was cut off by the slamming of the door. Tweedle Dee climbed in beside her.

Bobby got in the front and reached back to yank her purse away from her. He dug inside and pulled out her car keys. "Follow us in her car," Bobby said and threw the keys to Tweedle Dumb. He nodded and got out of the passenger seat and slammed the door.

Bobby put the van in drive, and they left Ohana's. Mia wanted to scream, to fight, but there was no way she could overpower the man beside her. He was large in every sense of the word. She didn't stand a chance. Glancing at the door, she wondered if could she pull it open and jump out. One look out the windshield told her they were on the main road now and going way too fast for her to survive throwing herself out of the speeding vehicle.

Shit. Shit. Shit. What the hell was she supposed to do now?

She bit her lip to curb her panic. It was one thing to talk big when Bobby wasn't in the room. It was a whole other ballgame now that he was holding her hostage in the back of a van. All she wanted at this point was to survive. And from the way Bobby kept glancing at her in the rearview mirror, that possibility was getting further and further away.

CHAPTER 5

CARTER WATCHED the van pull out and memorized the plate. The large black-haired guy with a lot of tattoos got into what Carter assumed was Mia's car and followed the van out. He'd only caught the very end of whatever happened, but it was enough to make his stomach churn.

When he'd started out of the bar, Mia was getting into the van. To be fair, it was more like she was being forced into the vehicle. He couldn't tell exactly what was going on from his angle and only moonlight for illumination, but he didn't think it was anything good. He'd kill for a pair of night vision goggles. His gut said there was an issue and if he trusted nothing else, he trusted that.

Carter hustled to his borrowed SUV, jumped in, and fired it up. Gravel crunched under the tires as he sped after the car and van. He'd caught up with them just as they reached the main road. He let them both pull out ahead of him and then let another car go by before following.

It was dark, and he hoped that whoever was driving the van and Mia's car wasn't really looking for a tail because with only one car between them, his headlights wouldn't be hard to spot.

They wound their way through town and into a neighborhood. The car ahead of him turned off leaving him fully exposed. Carter swore and dropped back. He kept the taillights of Mia's car in view but then lost them around a turn. His heart rate ticked up. He didn't know this woman from Adam, but seeing her get forced into that van caused major anxiety to tighten his chest. He sped up, but by the time he got around the corner, both vehicles had vanished.

"Fuck," he growled as he scanned the street. His heart rate kicked up another notch. Where the hell had they gone? The street was still. No cars moving. He put his window down and stopped. Was that car doors slamming? Instinct told him it was, and he peered at his surroundings. A small lane on the right veered off the roadway, heading up an incline. They must have gone up there. He killed his lights, reversed, and then took the hidden lane going up the hill. He crested the top and glanced in both directions. The van was parked in front of a small white house. The car was in the driveway.

Carter pulled onto the street and parked facing the opposite way. It was a risk if he needed to chase them but he didn't want to park next to them just in case he needed to follow them some more.

Carter watched the house in his rearview mirror. Maybe Mia wasn't in trouble. Maybe everything was fine, and he would look like some kind of weird stalker. He took a deep breath. *And maybe not.* He'd go with his gut on this one. Hopefully, this was all a misunderstanding and Mia would be okay with him following her.

Right now, he was helpless when it came to the investigation into what was going on with the other guys on the team. He couldn't stand by and do nothing here as well. He fucking hated being helpless.

Carter waited a couple of minutes and then got out of the SUV and made his way quickly to the van. Peering inside he found what he expected. It was empty. He glanced at the little house. The lights were on, but every window was covered. He had no idea if anyone was inside but he was betting that's where they'd taken Mia.

He opened the mailbox at the end of the driveway and pulled out a piece of mail. It was addressed to Mia. So it was her house. Carter moved swiftly up the driveway sticking to the dark shadows in case any neighbors happened to be looking out their windows. The last thing he needed was to be reported as a peeping tom. He crept to the side of the house. Sticking close to the wall, he slid up to a window and glanced in. An empty bathroom. He moved to the next window and risked a quick glance in. Kitchen. The lanky man who'd been driving had his back to the window. The two large guys, one with two full sleeves of tattoos and one with tattoos on his neck, were standing on either side of Mia. He didn't know her, but her expression told him she was pissed off and more than a little scared.

He took another quick peek. The two men were facing the window, so he had to be careful. Moving to the end of the building, he checked around the back of the little house. The small yard was taken up by a concrete patio with some grass beyond. Sliding glass doors led from the patio into the house. The doors were closed but thankfully, no curtains covered the opening.

Carter moved along the wall, ducking under a second kitchen window, and approached the glass doors. He cocked his head, heard them talking. He couldn't make out their words, though. Glancing around he quickly noted the kitchen window was raised a crack.

"Don't do anything stupid, Mia," the first voice said. "We're in this together now. If I go down, you go down. You're the accountant. They'll look at you when those books come to light."

"You asshole!" Mia's vehement cry cut through the night. "I was doing the fake books. I had no idea you were laundering money through the cafè."

"That don't matter now, does it?" Didn't need to see the guy's face to catch the sneer Carter knew would be on it. He continued, "If anyone says anything, I'll tell them you were in on the whole thing. And don't think I won't take down Akela and Kai, too."

"What the fuck do you want, Bobby?" Mia demanded. "There's no way you're just after my silence. You always want something."

The man named Bobby laughed. "You always were a smart one. Okay, Mia, I do want something. I want you to go back to start gambling for me again. I need you to win me some money."

Silence greeted these words and then, "No way. Not going to do it. I'm not going back to that, Bobby. I'm out. I'm done with that world. Hell will freeze over before I go back."

There was the sound of a scrape and then Mia let out a yelp. Carter's blood iced, and every SEAL instinct in him kicked to life. They were hurting Mia and he was fucking going to stop it. Now.

Carter ducked back under the window and hurried back toward the front of the house. He paused to look into the kitchen window one more time. The tall guy had Mia by the jaw and he was all up in her face.

Carter's gut rolled as he headed for the front of the house. He couldn't let this continue. Three against one wasn't great odds, and chances were good that these guys had a gun or two. But he'd also bet they were all slow. Big guys usually were. They used their size to intimidate people and rarely had to do any serious fighting.

He climbed the front steps as quietly as possible and then paused at the front door. Ever so gently, he tried the front door. The knob turned easily in his hand and opened just a fraction. He drew in a deep breath and then pushed the door open. "Mia, they didn't have any…" he let the words die out as he entered the house and took in the scene before him. "What the hell is going on?" he demanded.

The three men stared at him. The guy Carter assumed was Bobby dropped his hand from Mia's face and she swung her head in his direction as well, with her eyes full of confusion.

"Mia, honey, what's going on?" Carter demanded as he moved into the room. He positioned himself so he could take out the guy with the neck tattoos first and then Bobby. The guy with the full sleeves was on the far side of Mia and there was no way to reach him without going through her at this moment.

"I—I—"

"Whoever the fuck you are, you need to leave," Bobby demanded.

Carter shot him a look. "I'm Mia's boyfriend and I think you need to leave." He moved further into the room and got ready for a fight.

"You all need to leave," Mia said flatly. She tried to pull her arms from the two giants in the kitchen and they started to resist, but Bobby shook his head.

"Fine," Bobby said, "but this isn't over. Keep your mouth shut until we can talk some more. You feel me? Akela and Kai's lives depend on it." He cocked his head back in a way that made Carter want to cock his arm and throat-punch the asshole.

Mia said nothing but she remained still as Bobby and the two jacked-up bros with him moved slowly out of the little house.

Once the door was closed and locked behind them, she turned to Carter. "What in the hell are you doing here?"

Carter gave her the once over. "I saw the way you were manhandled into that van. Are you okay?"

"I'm fine." She stared at him. "Did you follow us here?"

"Yeah. Like I said, I saw you get into the van and had a bad feeling about it." He let his eyes roam over her. There were no outward signs of physical harm other than two red splotches on her cheeks where Bobby had held her face. That was enough to make him want to put the man six feet under. No one should treat a woman that way. Not ever. "Who were those guys?"

"It doesn't matter who they were. You can go, too." Mia started back toward the front door.

"Mia, you're obviously in trouble. Let me help you."

She turned and met Carter's gaze. "Look, I owe you one, okay? You saved my butt, but I have to deal with this stuff on my own. I don't need you sticking your nose in. It will just complicate things and they're complicated enough."

"Mia, I think I can help—"

"Carter, is it?" she asked as she frowned at him. "I barely know you. Now I appreciate you coming to my rescue, but things are way more complicated than they seem. And I do not need you in the middle of it, making it worse. So..." She walked over and unlocked the door, opening it wide. "Please leave."

Carter stood there and stared at the petite woman in front of him. He wanted to argue. To explain that it went against his nature to leave if she was in trouble. But he'd seen that look on his sister and mother's faces enough to know he was not going to win this argument. He was going to lose this battle. The important thing was to figure out how to win the war.

"Okay, but reach out if I can do anything to

help. I didn't like the way those men manhandled you." He started passed her and then stopped. "I mean it. I'm tougher than you think. I can handle a whole lot. Let me help you."

She just stared at him, so he dropped a quick kiss on her hair and went out the door. She closed it after him and he waited on her front porch until he heard the snick of the lock engaging. Then he headed back to his SUV. The van was gone, but Carter knew whatever trouble Mia was in, it wasn't likely to go away.

He just had to figure out a way to get her to let him help her. He had a feeling that if she didn't get some kind of help, things would go very badly for her. A likelihood he wanted to avoid at all costs. Mia had captured his attention, and he wasn't about to let anything happen to her. Not if he could help it.

CHAPTER 6

MIA PAUSED at the entryway into Kehola's gym and scanned the crowd. The great thing about growing up around here was she knew who to ask when she wanted to locate Akela. Her assistant from the café said she'd be at the gym watching Kai's session with his physical therapist. There was only one place on the island that Kai would go, so it was a no-brainer.

Akela was in the far corner, sitting on a yoga ball, watching her brother stretch. As Mia made her way across the floor, she took several deep cleansing breaths and tried to remind herself to be calm. Screaming at Akela wouldn't help keep the situation under wraps. The last thing she needed was for anyone to find out what the hell had been going on at the café. She'd been calling

Akela since seven a.m., but the other woman wouldn't pick up. Since Akela was maintaining radio silence, Mia had been forced to track her down. A fact that soured an already pissed-off mood.

"Akela." Mia's voice held a bit of a bark as she came to a stop in front of the other woman.

"What the hell?" Akela looked up, her large eyes startled. "You scared me."

Mia dropped her voice. "I'm about to do a lot more than scare you. We need to talk."

"Hey, Mia," a voice called from behind her.

She turned. "Hey, Kai. Looking good," she offered him a smile. Kai was a nice kid and he didn't deserve what happened to him. So few people did. Turning back to Akela, Mia said, "You've been avoiding my calls all morning. We're gonna talk now. Do you want to do it here in front of your brother and the rest of the world, or are you going to get up and come with me?"

Akela paled slightly and then glanced around. She stood up. "Fine." Turning to Kai, she waved. "I'm going to get a coffee with Mia. Back in a bit."

"Yeah, no worries. I'll be here." Kai went back to stretching.

The two women crossed the workout space

toward the little coffee shop that was in the corner of the gym. After they both ordered, they took their Americanos to a table in the back.

"What the fuck?" Mia snarled.

Akela blinked and bit her lip. "What? What's wrong?"

"Don't even try to play me, Akela. I know you told Bobby that I knew about the second set of books. He kidnapped me from Ohana's last night and then drove me home and threatened me."

Akela's face paled. "I'm so sorry." Her whispered apology was barely audible. "I didn't have a choice." A single tear trickled down her cheek and she quickly brushed it away. "Someone at work told him you'd been by and that you'd gone in the back room by yourself. One of my staff is a spy for Bobby. I didn't know. I swear it. I had no idea. I don't even know who it is. Anyway, he was at my house when I got home from seeing you. He threatened Kai. What was I supposed to do?"

Mia stared at her friend. She really did understand and might have done the same thing if the situation had been reversed. But, honestly, she didn't think she'd ever give up a friend that way. She blew out a breath. "He wants me to go back to my old life. He's threatening to start a rumor that I'm cooking your books. It would ruin my reputation and kill my livelihood."

"I'm so sorry, Mia. I truly am but what was I supposed to do?" Akela asked again.

"You should've known better from the beginning and then none of us would be in this mess," Mia snapped. She rubbed her face. That wasn't fair. She'd made mistakes with Bobby too. "Sorry." Her shoulders slumped. "That was harsh. I know how persuasive Bobby can be and I know how much you love Kai." She stared at her former teammate. "But Bobby wants me to start gambling again to make him money. I...I just don't want to go down that road."

Akela gripped her coffee mug as if she was freezing and the paper cup was the only thing that could keep herself warm. "I don't see a way out. If there was one, I'd take it." She met Mia's gaze. "You know that, right? If there was any other way, I'd do it?"

Mia's stomach sank. "Wait, you deliberately told him, didn't you? You told him that I could earn his money back."

Dull pink washed up Akela's cheeks. "I didn't have a choice. Bobby says the only way out for me is if I pay him one hundred thousand. That's what I owe him."

"Are you serious?" Mia swallowed hard. "A hundred thousand? He expects me to win him a hundred thousand dollars?"

Akela hesitated. "More. He needs money. A lot of it."

Mia stared across the table. "Did he tell you that?" Why in the hell would Bobby confide in Akela? *Shit.* Were they dating? "Are you with Bobby?"

Akela's mouth dropped open. "What? No way!" she said loudly and then immediately glanced around to see if anyone was paying attention. "No way," she repeated in a quieter, but still vehement voice. "I heard him and Donny talking. Bobby is laundering money for someone. I don't know who. Knowing him, I think he's even skimming some. He's trying to set up again. He lost everything when he went to prison, and now he's trying to rebuild. He said to Donny that he was tired of being told what to do. Now that he's been out for two years, he claims he's done taking orders. Whoever is running things right now doesn't like him, or trust him, or something because they won't let him in. He thinks if he gets more money he can branch out."

It was Mia's turn to stare. That was an awful lot of information for Akela to have if she wasn't dating Bobby. "Are you sure you're not together with Bobby, or maybe Donny?"

Akela shook her head. "Voices carry from the vent in my office to the one behind the counter. I overheard Bobby talking to Donny. He wants to take a run at whoever the boss is, but he needs more money to do it. He's pissed off about being held down. Bobby has big plans to take over the whole gambling ring or whatever the hell he's a part of. But he needs enough money to buy guns and whatever else he needs."

Mia sat back in her chair. "Are you sure?"

Akela nodded. "Yeah, I'm sure. Bobby is pissed that he's not calling the shots like he used to be. He said he's already paid his dues and now is his time. He wants back in the game. That's why he wants the money so badly."

Mia stared at her coffee. She had no interest in drinking it. Her stomach had already turned sour. "What did he tell you exactly?"

Akela tucked her hair behind an ear. "He said that I owe him one hundred thousand dollars. If I give him that we'll be even."

"But how is that going to stop the money laundering at the café? If he's not in charge then how is he going to stop it?"

She shrugged. "He thinks that once he has the

money that I owe him and whatever else he wants you to win for him, he can take over and be in charge again."

Mia frowned. "Do you believe him?"

Akela paused and then shook her head. "No, but what choice do I have? At least if he gets his money, maybe he'd forget about me, and I can rebuild my business. Once he stops hanging out, then people will come back. I know they will."

Mia wasn't sure that was true but that was Akela's problem, not Mia's. Her problem was Bobby. He thought she was his ticket to making money. "Does Bobby think I'll help you get the money because we're friends? Is that it? And he's just threatening me to ensure that I do it?"

"He's desperate. He's not gonna say anything about you to anyone because it would cause him problems if the boss finds out. But, Mia, if you don't do it, he *will* hurt Kai."

Mia ground her teeth as frustration burst behind her eyeballs. She really wanted to walk out of there and go see Emery. Tell her the whole thing and let the chips fall where they may. But seeing the terror on Akela's face, she knew she couldn't do that. She'd been stupid before and managed to get out of it without too much damage. Or so she'd thought until her parents died. The cops still believed it was an accident, but Mia wasn't so sure. Bobby had vowed revenge, and it probably wasn't coincidence that her parents' accident had happened so soon after he'd gotten out of prison. She'd tortured herself about being the root cause of the accident on and off for the last two years.

"Why has it taken Bobby two years to get fed up? He doesn't seem like the patient sort. Why now? What's going on that he wants to make his move now?"

Akela shrugged. "I've no idea and I don't really care. I just want to be done with this." She pushed her cup away. "Will you do it? Will you play again?"

Mia stared across the table. She wanted to say no but she couldn't if it meant someone innocent, like Kai, could be hurt. "Let me think about it." She stood up. "I'll be in touch."

With that, she left the gym and walked out into the sunshine. Cold seemed to have seeped into her bones as she sat with Akela and now it was glorious to be out in the warmth. Too bad the sun couldn't burn away garbage like Bobby. She was stuck with him.

Mia got in her vehicle and then drove home. It was Saturday and she usually spent the day sorting out paperwork. Today, with nervous energy to burn, she cleaned her house until it was spotless, trying to erase any trace that Bobby and his goons had been there. Then she made some cookies and a lasagna for the week—anything to keep her hands and her mind busy. She did not want to think about the problem at hand.

Finally, with all of her chores finished and the afternoon stretching before her, Mia sat down at her dining table and started on the paperwork. She didn't last ten minutes before jumping to her feet to pace. Setting aside the problem of Bobby, there was another issue. The reason Mia didn't gamble anymore was because she liked it. She liked it a lot.

A sudden knock at the door startled her. Heart doing a two-step in her chest, she checked the peep hole. *Carter. Shit.* Would this guy never give up? She opened the door. "What do you want?"

He studied her face. "Nice to see you, too."

She frowned.

"I brought food." He held up a brightly colored bag. "Tacos."

She recognized the bag from her favorite taco place. Her stomach rumbled as she caught a whiff. Lasagna was fine but tacos were much better. "Fine," she said less than graciously as she backed up and let him in.

"I'll take it," Carter said with a grin.

She walked over and cleared the papers off the table and gestured for him to sit down. Then she went about getting plates and cutlery. "Do you want something to drink?"

"I'll have whatever you're having." She nodded and got out a bottle of wine. She poured herself and Carter glasses of the dry white wine and carried them to the table.

Mia sat down and Carter handed her a couple of tacos. She nodded her thanks and put them on her plate but didn't unwrap them immediately. She suddenly realized she owed this man a thank you. He'd come to her rescue last night and she'd been less than grateful for it.

"About last night. I just want to say thank you. It was…a tense situation and you helped. I guess I owe you one."

Carter gave her an appraising look and she couldn't help but notice his blue eyes. They really were spectacularly blue, like the sky at twilight. His t-shirt stretched across his chest in a way that made her want to see more and if she was truly being honest, he had the nicest ass. She'd noticed it when he'd walked across the room in front of her. None of those things were helpful but they sure made him easy on the eyes.

"You know what you can do to pay me back?"

"Surfing. Yes, I'll teach you." She smiled and then started unwrapping her taco.

"Well, that too, but I'd rather you tell me what the hell is going on with that guy and his goons."

She froze. It hadn't occurred to her that Carter was going to want to know more about the situation last night, but it should've. Stupid. If she hadn't been distracted by those eyes and the tacos, then she would've been smart enough to tell him no when he said he wanted to come in.

She narrowed her eyes at him. "It's none of your business."

He cocked his head. "True, but it appears to me that you're in trouble. And chalk this up to my savior complex, but I'd like to help."

"I don't need help." God, the last thing she needed was to involve anyone else in this mess.

"I beg to differ. You needed my help last night and you're gonna need it again. That guy isn't going away, is he? He wants you to do something for him. Something you don't want to do. I can help you."

She pushed her chair back from the table and

stood. "Carter, I appreciate what you did last night, and I thank you for dinner. I will teach you to surf, but I need you to stay out of my business. It doesn't concern you. I can take care of myself. Please leave."

He stood and started to say something when his cell phone went off. He pulled it out, glanced at the screen, and closed his mouth. His expression went blank. "I've got to take this. But this isn't over, Mia. You need help that I can provide. Take advantage of me. I don't want to see you get hurt." He leaned over and kissed her on the cheek and then he was gone, leaving her staring after him. What the hell just happened and why did she suddenly feel so alone?

CHAPTER 7

"CASTLE CALLED," Carter said as he turned onto the ranch road. "Tell the other two and meet me at my cabin. I'm just pulling in now."

Bowie grunted, "On it," and then hung up.

Carter parked the Jeep and climbed out, grabbing the bag of groceries from the back seat. He'd left Mia's when Castle called and stopped for a few supplies on the way back.

Ten minutes later, the sound of boots on the outside steps announced the arrival of his team. Bowie pulled open the screen door. "Yo, you got any beer?"

Carter, who had just finished putting everything away, opened the fridge again and handed Bowie a beer. "You two want one?" he asked.

Flint and Quinn nodded as they crashed

down on the chairs around the dining table that overlooked the ranch. The view was excellent, with the rolling hills and the ocean in the distance, but it was the last thing on anyone's mind.

"Don't keep us in suspense, brother. What did Castle say?" Quinn asked.

Carter opened his beer and sat down. "He's found a lead that could connect McCarthy, Hendrick, Jones, and Ferrero to dirty money. Castle visited the widows of the previous team members. He asked them if anything was out of the ordinary or stood out to them. One of them, not sure who, handed him a file that her husband had collected on McCarthy and the others. It turns out her husband had been suspicious for a while. He told her they had too much money and were flashing it around. He knew for a fact they had a lake house somewhere that was much more expensive than any of them could afford, even if they all went in together. He saw pictures of it in Henrick's cage."

"So we're right. Those boys are on the take." Flint's grunt sounded a lot like disgust.

A sentiment Carter agreed with.

"Yeah, and they killed their team members," Bowie pointed out.

Quinn slammed his bottle on the table. "These guys need to go down. Hard."

"Agreed," Carter said and then continued. "Castle said that he found a company named Cerberus in the file the woman gave him and he's trying to track it down. He thinks it's important."

"Why is that familiar?" Bowie asked.

Quinn cocked his head. "Yeah, it's ringing faint bells. Why do we know it?"

Flint snapped his fingers. "It's McCarthy's favorite dog's name."

"Shit," Carter growled, "that's right." He grabbed his phone and sent a text to his CO. "Castle said this is a shell company, but he's tracing it, and he's pretty sure this will lead directly back to them. The big question is; are they the only ones involved?"

Flint stared. "You think there are more teams involved in this shit?"

Carter shook his head. "Not teams. I think someone higher up the chain of command must be involved. Otherwise, how do they get to these locations? They don't get to pick their targets. Orders come from higher up the chain of command, so it's got to be someone with power enough to send them where they need to be to steal the money and drugs."

"You're back to thinking it's Castle's boss, Fuller," Quinn stated.

Carter nodded.

"Makes sense," Bowie acknowledged. "What does Castle say?"

"Not much just yet, but I think he's thinking the same thing. He knows it has to be someone at his level or above to wield that kind of power. Since he knows he's not involved, it limits who it could be." Carter leaned back in his chair. "He told us to hang tight. Continue doing testing, and then if he can't get it sorted quickly, he'll find somewhere else to send us. He also promised not to send us overseas with McCarthy and the rest again until he figured this out."

"So we're here for the foreseeable future," Bowie said. "I like the sound of that. I love Hawai'i."

"You're loving the good-lookin' women and good food," Quinn commented.

"And like you're not?" Bowie countered.

Quinn grinned. "I didn't say that."

Flint finished his beer. "It's definitely a step up from the last place we were stationed. I could get used to this, no question."

Carter took a sip of his beer and thought of Mia. He could get used to things here, too, but maybe that wasn't a good thing. "So, what do we do?" he asked.

"Just what the man says," Quinn replied. "We continue the testing and enjoy Hawai'i. God only knows where we'll get sent after this. We might as well enjoy being here while we can."

"I'll drink to that," Flint agreed. "Carter, get me another beer."

LATER THAT EVENING, after a rousing game of poker, his teammates left, and Carter couldn't sleep. His mind kept circling around over what Castle had said. He was making progress but would it be enough? And if he didn't find something to connect Fuller, then what would happen? Edward Fuller III had never been one of his favorite people, but before this Carter never would have thought the man could be crooked.

Suppose Castle could only bring down McCarthy, Hendrick, Jones, and Ferrero but couldn't connect the dots to Fuller? Then what would happen to them? Would Fuller still send them overseas and get them killed somehow? Were there any scenarios where they could get McCarthy and his boys to flip on Fuller, or whoever pulled their strings? Fuller had a hell of a lot of power in the Navy. Be hard to take that on. He worried for his CO. Castle was risking his career to save Carter and the team. In the end, would it be enough? Would Castle be found out and would Fuller try to have the others kill him?

Carter scrubbed a fist over his chest. This wasn't helping him. He needed to let it go. At the moment, he was powerless. The helpless feeling roused memories of his dad's death. There was nothing he could do to save his father as the man died right in front of him. He'd had a widow-maker heart attack and even though Carter had done CPR, there was no way he could bring his father back. Feeling helpless always brought back that memory and it haunted him. He needed to find something here in Hawai'i to amuse him. Something to keep him busy and stop the constant cycle of futile thinking.

He deliberately turned his thoughts away from his father and turned them to Mia. That was a situation he might be able to sink his teeth into. He'd like to sink his teeth into Mia but thinking like that wasn't helpful either. He'd just end up with blue balls. The stunning woman was in trouble and it had something to do with gambling, which was illegal in Hawai'i. If only she'd open up to him. He might be able to help or at least protect her. That guy Bobby was bad news, and he didn't need any kind of background intel to know it.

He thought about the license plate on the van. Maybe he'd ask Hawk tomorrow to run it. Also, he would pick the guy's brain about Bobby whatever his name was and illegal gambling here on the Big Island. If Mia refused to trust him, he could come at the problem from the other direction. If he could figure out Bobby, then maybe he could stop him before Mia got involved more deeply.

With that decided, Carter rolled over and started the breathing exercise the military had taught him to get to sleep in less-than-ideal conditions. He might not be able to do anything about the situation with McCarthy and his boys but maybe, just maybe, he could help Mia. And that would make all the difference in the world to him.

CHAPTER 8

"Two hundred and fifty thousand? Are you out of your mind?" Mia stared at Bobby, her mouth hanging open. Akela only owed him a hundred K. How could he want her to raise another hundred and fifty thousand?

"That's what you need to make me," Bobby affirmed as he stood with his arms folded across his chest.

"You're crazy!" Mia blurted out. "I know Akela and Kai don't owe you that much."

"I didn't say that's what they owe me. I said that's what you need to make me if you want me to leave them and you alone."

She glared at him. "You fucker. You're just trying to make it outrageous so I can't ever pay you back."

Bobby shook his head. "No, you're gonna do it and you've only got a couple of weeks to make it happen. I don't have time for you to screw around."

Mia's voice cracked. "Are you insane? There's no game in town where I can make that in a couple of weeks. I mean even back when you were running things, I'd be lucky to walk away with twenty grand after a week of playing black-jack every night."

Bobby glanced out at the water. "Yeah, well things are different now. I'm not running the games anymore and the stakes are much bigger than they used to be."

"Who the hell is running things?" Mia demanded.

Bobby took a step closer and got in her face. "It doesn't matter who it is. You work for me. You're gonna do this or suffer the consequences. Do you hear me?"

Mia wanted to slap the menacing look off Bobby's face. She hated this man and she couldn't believe she was about to do his bidding. It made her want to puke. "How am I supposed to make that kind of money?"

"I'm gonna give you the address of a gaming locale. You're gonna put a dress on that hot little body of yours and show up and play blackjack. You're gonna make enough to catch the eye of the guy who runs the place. He goes by Peter. Once you catch his eye, he's gonna invite you to the real games where big money is on the line and that is where you're gonna win me two hundred and fifty grand. Once you do that, you and Akela and her brother are all free as birds."

Instinctively, Mia knew that Bobby was lying to her. They'd never be free. He'd never let her walk away if she could win him that kind of money. But she was between a rock and the proverbial hard place, with no option except to comply with his demands. She was going to play. Hopefully, she would figure something out as she was making the money. She swore silently. That was a shit ton of money and only having two weeks to do it was daunting.

"What do you need the money for?" Mia asked. She figured what the hell? Maybe he'd tell her something that might help her out somehow.

"None of your fucking business."

"I know you're trying to get your place back on the island. Time in jail really screwed up your hold on things. Looks like you're out in the cold still after two long years." And she was certain this freeze-out was pissing him all the way off.

Bobby slammed his fist on the top of the car next to her, and she shivered involuntarily. "Don't push me, Mia, or I might decide you're not worth the hassle and kill you myself."

Mia bit her tongue to hold her retort in. She didn't think Bobby would kill her, at least not until he got his money. Then all bets were off. "Fine. I'm going to need buy-in money."

"It's a grand and you need to supply it."

Mia demanded. "You are insane. What makes you think I have a grand lying around that I can use to gamble with?"

Bobby leaned in again. "You better because I'm not supplying it. You're an accountant, work some magic with some numbers and pull the money out of a hat. I don't care how you do it but be at this address tonight by ten p.m. Look for Peter. I'll tell him you're coming. You better start earning because you don't have much time." With that, Bobby pushed away from the car and stomped across the parking lot to where two guys waited in an SUV. He climbed into the back, and they peeled out, accompanied by squealing tires.

Shoulders bunched high toward her ears, Mia watched them go. How the hell had she gotten herself involved in this mess? More importantly, how the hell was she going to get out of it?

MIA TUGGED at the short black cocktail dress. The hemline was higher than she'd like but Bobby had warned she'd have to dress to fit in with the gambling crowd. He'd been right. Calling her current location a backroom gambling den made it sound cheap and tawdry, with bad lighting and worse people. While she couldn't attest to the people, the surroundings were anything but tawdry.

When Bobby had called a bit ago, to be sure she was on her way, she'd almost told him to fuck off. But at the last second, she'd stopped herself from deliberately baiting him. She wasn't doing this so much for Akela and Kai, although they played a role, but more for herself. Maybe there was a way to get Bobby arrested again. Not to mention, he really could wreck her reputation and that would put her out of business.

She arrived at the address Bobby had supplied and was amazed by what she found. This upscale site wasn't one of his usual back-room games. The building was a warehouse in the industrial district, but once she'd been allowed in, all thoughts of this being a warehouse vanished. Inside, it had been all dolled up. The walls had been blacked out with curtains and the vast floor was covered in flashy red carpet. The people there probably surprised her the most. All manner of attire clothed the guests. Everything from evening gowns and tuxedos to jeans and tank tops. One guy was even barefoot and wearing only board shorts. She shook her head.

A server came by and offered Mia a glass of champagne. She declined. As much as she wanted to down a glass or three, she knew she needed to keep her wits about her. Surreptitiously wiping her sweaty palms on her dress, she studied the room. There were several poker tables and even a roulette wheel, but she was searching for blackjack. That was her thing. She could play poker, but it wasn't her strength. She hated having the decisions other people made affect her chances of winning. Before when she'd played, Bobby knew that and had allowed her to have a table with a dealer all to herself. Back then he hadn't run the small back room shit he was running today. Back before he went to prison, his operation was more upscale, not quite to this level, but closer to this than what he was doing now. He really had come down in the world. And now he wanted back up and apparently, she was supposed to be his ticket.

"Ms. Ryan." A tall gentleman with well-groomed hair and high cheekbones approached her. He was very attractive and offered her a smile. "Mr. Kamaka said you might be dropping by."

"I see," she said. What was she supposed to say now? I want a table to myself. There was no way they were going to offer that until she proved her ability, which meant she had hours of playing ahead of her. She was going to have to establish herself all over again. She'd asked Bobby why she couldn't just play at his back-room games, but apparently, the only game he offered was poker. *How the mighty have fallen.*

"I'm Peter. Can I interest you in a seat at one of our tables?"

"I think I'll just get the lay of the land first if that's okay." She offered him a small smile.

"Of course. Did Mr. Kamaka explain that the buy-in is one thousand dollars?"

She swallowed. She'd wanted to choke him when he'd demanded she supply the funds. To be honest, she still wanted to choke him. "Yes."

Peter lifted his arm. "You may purchase your

chips over there when you are ready." He pointed towards a high counter where three women stood behind big plexiglass slabs with just enough room at the bottom to exchange money for chips.

She nodded and headed toward the counter. By her rough estimate, there were upwards of sixty people in the room. She recognized several of the top businessmen from the island and their wives. There was even a software giant who owned a house on the island. This little shindig was a Who's Who of the rich on the Big Island. Whoever was running this site had major pull.

Bobby didn't have that kind of juice, not even in his heyday. She didn't think two hundred and fifty thousand was going to be enough for him to step in and take over this level of gaming.

That made her wonder what he was really trying to do. What was his goal?

As she exchanged her cash for chips, she was curious about the buy-in. It was low for this kind of crowd. Why would it be kept low? Mia wandered about the room, carefully watching the players. Then it hit her. Yes, there were bigwigs in the room, but the vast majority of players were people like her. People who wanted to play but weren't super wealthy. She even spotted her dry cleaner.

This was what Bobby wanted. Not the high rollers, but the bread and butter crowd. People who maybe were barely making rent or buying groceries. Because that's what these people were. Underneath the flash, this was just the middle class set, for lack of a better word. And Mia was willing to bet they came every week. Suddenly, this gambit made more sense. If Bobby hooked those people, then he would be raking it in and he wouldn't have to fork out for champagne and fancy surroundings.

Mia finally made her way over to the black-jack table in the corner, where three other players were hunched over their cards. She watched them for a while and determined that only the woman on the end in the green sequined gown was good. She knew what she was doing and, judging by the stack of chips in front of her, was making some serious money. The man next to her in the tux was too drunk to pay any real attention to what he was doing, and the other gentleman at the far end wore chinos, a button down, and an air of desperation. The pile of chips in front of him was quickly diminishing.

Mia waited until the dealer, a young pretty

blonde, opened a new deck. Then she grabbed the chair between the two men. The dealer, whose name tag read Patty, recited the rules and the buy-in. Mia nodded and put a couple of chips on the table. The chink of the chips as she stacked them started her heart hammering against her rib cage. A surge of adrenaline shivered through her, left her skin clammy. She swallowed.

It had been years since she'd allowed herself to play. While she was rusty, almost certainly the knowledge would come back to her as soon as she sorted the cards she was dealt. That familiarity was her big worry. She hadn't quit gambling because she didn't like it, or she sucked at it. On the contrary, she'd quit because she liked the thrill of winning too much. She made a lot of money very quickly and she wanted more. It had taken her parents staging an intervention... forcing her to sit down and face the dark road she'd been headed down, to make her stop. By the time they said something, Mia was already sleeping during the day and only going out to gamble at night. She'd stopped seeing any friends and she had no life outside of blackjack.

She'd never wanted to go back to that lifestyle, but here she was.

Taking a deep breath as the dealer dealt her cards, Mia knew she had to clear her mind and concentrate fully on the table. It would be doubly hard with these other players to make the right calls and she had to be smart with her money. That was the only way she'd make enough to stand out to Peter, hoping for an invitation to the big games. For her sake, and Akela's and Kai's, that's what needed to happen. It would take her a month of Sundays to earn enough at a thousand-dollar table to pay off the two hundred and fifty thousand. There was a top limit of ten thousand.

The goal was to earn a seat at the high-stakes table and the only way she'd get there was by invitation. It was going to take some doing and a lot of playing, but most of all, it was going to take every inch of her concentration and smarts to do this right. Mia picked up her cards with a small prayer that she didn't screw up. If she didn't get the money, it was game over for all three of them. She did not want that on her conscience. Not if she could help it.

CHAPTER 9

Mia flopped down on her sofa, cup of coffee in her hand. It had been a long time since she'd pulled an all-nighter, and she was drained. Not only were her feet tired from being in spike heels all night, but her brain was toast from having to concentrate so hard on her game.

She'd been rustier than she'd thought, and it had taken her a while to find her groove again. Playing at the same table with other people hadn't helped. Ed, the guy in the tux was a disaster. He kept taking cards when he should have stayed, causing her to miss out on some good hands. After two hours of mediocre results, Ed had finally wandered off and then she managed to get things back on track. Once the other two had left the table as well, then it was game on.

She hadn't planned on staying all night but once she had the table to herself and she seriously started to concentrate, everything clicked into place. It was as if the years had fallen away, and she was right back in the thick of it again.

Not somewhere she ever dreamed she be again.

Staring at the cash on the coffee table in front of her, she swore out loud. Yes, Bobby wanted two hundred and fifty thousand to make all of her and Akela's problems go away, so it wasn't like she had a choice. But the truth of the matter was that she'd reveled in the second half of the night. The fact that she'd made ten grand in the first night did not help. She could make up what Bobby wanted in a month if she played conservatively. Of course, she didn't have a month which meant pushing the boundaries. *Not good at all.*

She sipped the steaming coffee and then set her mug down. She rubbed her bleary eyes. The situation was untenable. Mia picked up her phone and checked her calendar. She had lots of office visits scheduled for this week. Her real business demanded that she visit her clients at least once a month to make sure things were on track. They appreciated the personal touch, and it made her slightly higher rates easier to swallow. Her clients were paying her to be on call and they knew they could trust her to fix any problems and even catch some before they started.

And all that would go away if Bobby leaked that she'd been cooking the books for Akela.

She blew out a frustrated breath. No one would hire an accountant accused of cooking the books. Or at least no one she wanted to work for. Crap, that kind of information could even mean a visit from the cops. That was the last thing she wanted. Emery would find out and then Mia would be beyond embarrassed. She did not want Emery or any of her other friends to find out about any of this. Emery *and* Dahlia would be livid with Mia for not coming to tell them in the first place.

Mia took another sip of coffee and leaned back on the sofa. Was there an option to go to the cops? Not really. If she went to them, she figured they'd want her to continue what she was doing. For them having a person on the inside was huge.

But for her, being that inside person increased her personal danger level tenfold. If Bobby found out, he'd ruin her reputation unless, of course, he just flat-out killed her. She shuddered. Assuming he didn't end her life, if she defended herself by claiming she'd been working for the cops, then her clients wouldn't like it any better. How could they trust her to keep their secrets? Granted, no one was doing anything downright illegal but there were some gray areas where she was dabbling for certain clients who were willing to take a bit more risk. Nothing that could cause her trouble, but they could get their knuckles rapped if they were ever audited and things didn't swing their way. Those people would never trust her again and those people made up half her client list.

She looked around at her little dream house. She loved the warm gray walls with white accents. The light-colored wood floors with the white furniture and bright blue pillows. The mantel above the fireplace where she displayed pictures of her family and friends. This house was her piece of heaven, serving her joy every day. She'd taken great pains to decorate it and get it just right. And sure, there were issued that required repair or outright replacement, but this little house was the one place in the world where she was completely comfortable.

Or it had been until Bobby arrived. No, she wouldn't let him ruin it for her. This was her happy spot, and no one would take that from her, not even Bobby with all his threats.

But, she had to be realistic. He had the power to destroy what she'd built and working with the cops would not make it better. In fact, it would be worse. More danger for her, and prison time for Akela. She resented her friend for dragging her into this mess but there was no way she wanted to be responsible for sending the other woman to prison. She understood why Akela had done what she had. If the situation was reversed, Mia wasn't sure she wouldn't do the same thing.

A knock at the door had her jumping to her feet and spilling coffee on the floor. *What the hell? What now?* She swore as she put her mug down on the coffee table and then went to the kitchen to grab a kitchen towel.

"Coming," she called as she quickly wiped up the spill and then stared at the cash stacked neatly on the table. Where the hell was she going to put that? The knock sounded again. Mia quickly grabbed the bills and stuffed them under the sofa cushions. She straightened, looking around frantically but nothing else appeared out of place.

She headed to the door and glanced through the peephole, letting out a quiet curse once she identified the man standing on the other side.

"What are you doing here?" she asked as she opened the door.

"Good morning to you too, Mia." Carter's smile was warm and sexy and it hit her like a jolt of electricity. Her damn toes curled.

"Sorry." She willed the heat out of her cheeks. "Long night. Good morning, Carter. How are you?" She added a simpering smile to eradicate the grumble in her tone.

"I'm doing well. I thought maybe I could catch you before you left for work." He held up a paper bag

"Are you always going to show up with food?" Mia demanded as the smell hit her and her stomach rumbled loudly.

His smile broadened. "Hungry, huh?"

Mia wanted to say no but damn it, she was starving, and the food smelled so good. She turned away from the door. No point in denying it. Her stomach had been so loud, she wouldn't be surprised if her neighbors had heard it. She made her way to the kitchen fighting the embarrassment she knew was coloring her cheeks still.

"Do you want coffee?" she asked. When she didn't get a response, she turned to find her kitchen empty. She went back around the corner and stared at Carter still standing on the step. "Are you coming?"

"You didn't invite me."

God, was he a freaking vampire that needed an invitation to cross the threshold. She shook her head. "That didn't stop you the other night." She bit her lip. *Shit.* She'd wanted to avoid that topic but the words had just shot out of her mouth.

"Extenuating circumstances? Now I need an invitation."

She snorted. "Seriously, are you a vampire?"

He barked out a laugh. "Good one, but no. I was just raised to respect a woman's wishes and never assume anything. Are you going to invite me in?"

Mia wanted to say something snarky but had to admit she was impressed. "Please come in, Carter. Would you like some coffee?"

"I'd love some," he said as he closed the door and toed off his boots.

Mia filled a mug for him, and refilled hers, then placed one in front of him at the island. She grabbed some cutlery and came around and sat down, handing him a knife and fork, and putting hers down with her coffee in front of her. "What did you bring me?"

"Loco Moco from a place in town. The guys at the ranch say it's the best."

"It is the best." Her stomach growled again. It was her favorite. "Have you had it before?"

Carter shook his head. "No, but given the way everyone sings its praise, I thought I'd give it a try."

Mia smiled. "You are in for a treat." She rose again and got plates and then dished out the food, placing a full plate in front of him.

Carter stared at it for a moment. "I can't remember ever eating rice for breakfast."

Mia took up her food and then went and sat down next to Carter. "Then you're missing out. This is heaven. Rice with a beef patty, and an egg on top smothered in gravy. It doesn't get better than this."

Carter forked the first bite into his mouth and chewed. He swallowed and then nodded. "Okay, it sounded weird to me, but damn, this is really good."

"Yup. It's outstanding." Mia took her first bite and savored it. She didn't allow herself to have Loco Moco very often, but it was her favorite breakfast. She used to go with her parents almost weekly when they were alive. She found herself suddenly blinking back tears. *Weird.* Must be because she was overtired.

The next minutes were spent in silence as they ate. Mia relished her breakfast and by the look of Carter's empty plate, so did he. "More coffee?"

"Sure." Carter pushed his mug in her direction. Then he stood, picked up the plates, and carried them to the kitchen.

"You don't have to do that," Mia said as she followed him.

"I don't mind." He rinsed the plates and then looked around. "Dishwasher?"

"I don't have one," she said with a sigh. It was on her list to install but the money just wasn't there for that kind of thing. It would involve redoing the entire kitchen because of the way things were laid out. Gambling like she had last night would help her earn the cash, but until she'd been forced back into it, she hadn't even given it a thought.

"Okay." He set them down in the sink and started looking around again.

"Just leave them. I'll get them later." He was annoying her. Suddenly, it felt as if her lack of a dishwasher was a mark against her. Having him in her small kitchen made her uncomfortable enough for altogether different reasons, and now she felt some kind of silent rebuke.

Carter turned and she handed him his coffee. "Here."

"Thanks. I don't have a dishwasher either. Never saw the need when there's only me." He flashed her a smile and took a sip of coffee as he leaned back against the counter. "Why is the coffee so much better on this island?"

Mia blinked. Damn that smile and its ability to slay her every time. And now she just felt stupid about the whole dishwasher thing. She was way too sensitive about her home. She sighed and then took a sip of her own coffee.

"So…" she began as she searched for some topic of conversation. "How long are you in town for? Dahlia mentioned you and your friends were visiting out at the ranch with Hawk.

"Yeah," Carter agreed, but he cocked his head as if asking how she knew that.

"It's a small town. A group of new guys showing up at Ohana's pretty much means we're all gossiping about you."

"Good to know. We're in town for a few weeks. We'll see how it goes. We're testing some equipment out at the ranch."

"You're in the military? Navy, is it?" Mia tried

to be casual about it. The way she'd heard it from one of Dahlia's texts, they were SEALs.

"Yeah," he said.

The corners of his lips curled slightly upward as if he knew she was trying to play it cool. *Shit.* She needed to get this man out of her house. He was messing with her mind. *Overtired.* That had to be it. She took another sip of coffee. It couldn't possibly be the fact that he was sexy as hell and standing in her kitchen giving her a look that made her toes curl and her lady parts tingle. Nope, it couldn't possibly be that.

CHAPTER 10

"You look great, by the way." Carter set his mug on the counter. He meant the compliment. She looked spectacular in the dress. It hugged all her curves and showed off her legs in a way that Carter felt below his belt. Damn if it wasn't super distracting. He needed to focus on the problem at hand. "But why do I have the feeling that you still being in a cocktail dress at eight in the morning has to do with those three goons who were here?"

Mia glanced down at her dress like she'd forgotten she was wearing it. "Forget it, Carter. Like I said before, I don't need your help. Thanks for breakfast but you know where the door is."

"Mia, you need help. I know it, and *you* know it. Whatever it is, you're in over your head."

She whirled around, her hands on her hips which was never a good sign. Carter braced himself for the coming storm.

"What makes you think I can't handle myself? I've been taking care of myself for years. I don't need you interfering in my life. Just because you bring me food doesn't mean you have any say in my life. Just. Butt. Out. Stop coming over. Forget where I live." She glared at him.

Carter kept his voice measured and his stance relaxed. Dealing with Mia reminded him of working with injured animals. Eliminate sudden or potentially threatening movements. *Proceed with caution.* "I'm sure you can take care of yourself in normal circumstances, but I also know that this isn't normal. Three men stood in your house and hurt you. This Bobby guy said you had to do what he wanted because two lives depended on it. None of that is normal. Whatever is going on, you need help. Please let me help you, Mia. I don't want to see anything bad happen to you."

"Too late." She let out a long sigh. "Look, I really appreciate that you want to help me. I truly do but you can't get involved in this. It's hard enough as it is, I don't need any further complications. So, thank you, but I think it's better if you don't stop by anymore." With that, she turned and headed around the corner.

He had no doubt she was standing by the door waiting for him to leave but he wasn't willing to give up just yet. Navy SEALs never quit. He moved toward her sofa. "I get that you're worried and you're in trouble. You don't want to make it worse, but Mia, my job in the Navy is basically dealing with trouble in all kinds of hell-holes around the world. I know what I'm doing, and I can handle myself, no question. I'm not afraid of a two-bit thug. More importantly, I can help you keep your friends safe. Let me. I can keep you safe and no matter what happens to me, I guarantee I won't hold you responsible."

Carter had no idea why he was so willing to get into the middle of whatever this was to help Mia, but he just knew that he was determined to keep her safe. If he had to guess it was probably a reaction to being holed up in Hawai'i while his CO tried to figure out what the hell was going on with the other half of the team. The last eight months had taken a larger toll than he was willing to admit. It was one thing to go out on an op with his teammates when he knew they had his back when the shit hit the fan. And it always did. It was another thing altogether to have to look over his shoulder to check for 'friendly fire' while at the same time fighting the known enemy in front of him.

The bottom line, he was tired of feeling help-less. Of not being able to do his job properly. Of not knowing if he could trust four members of the team who had sworn allegiance to each other. And now being out of the loop with the investigation, made him itchy. He wanted to be in a situation that he could control. That he could affect the outcome without worrying about someone supposedly on his side doing him in. He wanted a situation where he wasn't help-less and it was clear who the bad guys were.

"Mia, you need help and if I'm honest, I need something to do. There's a lot going on back on the mainland and currently I can't be a part of it. I'm not so good with that, so I need a distraction. You would be doing me a favor by letting me get involved. And I swear I can keep you safe and help with your friends." Okay, that last part might have been an exaggeration but at least he could try.

Mia bit her lip and dropped her hand from the doorknob as she studied him. A pounding on the door made her jump. She stared at it and all the color left her cheeks.

"Let me answer it." He rushed to her side. In a low voice, he said, "Go stand in the hallway out of sight."

She hesitated but then the pounding rattled the door again, and she nodded. Carter waited until she was no longer visible, then opened the door a bit and stood in the opening, blocking the view inside. "Hello. Bobby, is it?"

Bobby glared at him. "I want to see Mia. Now."

"She's busy." Carter kept the opening small and looked beyond Bobby to the two henchmen standing behind him.

"Well get her un-busy."

"No can do. You want to leave a message?"

"Yeah," Bobby said and then pushed forward expecting the door to open wider when he banged on it. The surprised expression on his face was nearly comical when he realized it didn't move because Carter's foot was blocking it and Bobby ended up crashing into the solid wood.

"Fuck," he snarled. "God damn get her for me now!"

"You're attracting attention," Carter pointed out as a woman who was walking her dog paused out in front of the house to watch them.

"Unless you want the cops to come, I suggest you leave. Quietly. I'll tell Mia you were here and ask her to call you."

Bobby turned to glare at the woman, who then hurried away, tugging her dog along. Bobby swore again as a car rolled slowly passed. "Fine. Tell her to call me ASAP. And if you fuck with me again, you'll regret it." He stomped down the steps with his two bruisers in tow.

Carter watched them go and when their van left the curb, he closed the door and locked it.

Mia came out of the hallway with her arms wrapped around her waist.

"Let me help you," he offered again.

She cocked her head and Carter knew she was considering his offer. *Say yes. Say yes*, he willed her.

"How can you think you can help me when you have no idea what I'm involved in."

Now we're getting somewhere. She was considering his offer. He could work with that. "You're right, but I'm a Navy SEAL. I'm pretty sure I can handle a few assholes who like to prey on women."

"What if it's more than that?"

Carter shrugged. "If I can't deal with it on my own, I have three other guys who will jump in to help me. We're part of a team. We stick together no matter what."

She swallowed and rubbed her face and then she chewed on her bottom lip. Carter had a hard time concentrating. His gaze zeroed in on her lips. *Focus*, he reminded himself, but she cocked her head, and her hair, which had been pinned up, fell down her back, and he immediately pictured tangling his hands in it. The urge to kiss Mia was so intense he missed her next words. "Sorry?" he mumbled.

"I said, I would have to pay you."

"Pay me?" The thought was insulting. "I don't want your money."

"You don't accept payment then we don't do this." She folded her arms across her chest.

Damn. He hadn't seen that coming. He gritted his teeth. "Fine, you can pay me." An idea came to him. "We can work it out in trade. You teach me how to surf and I will help you with your problem." He wasn't sure she was going to buy it. How much could surfing lessons cost?

She narrowed her eyes at him. "I'll tell you what's going on and you can decide if you truly want to get involved in this mess. If you don't, that's fine but you can't tell anyone, especially the cops. You do that and I'm dead. So are my friends."

It was a no-brainer. "Agreed."

Mia went over and sat down on the couch. *No sudden movements*. He took the matching chair on her right. "Tell me what's going on." He spied a hundred dollar bill sticking partially out from under the cushion. Carter said nothing but he knew whatever was coming was going to be much more interesting than he'd anticipated.

Mia spent a solid thirty minutes telling Carter her story. She was succinct and met his eyes. Two good signs. When people meandered in telling their tales, he often felt they were making it up as they went along.

"Bobby sounds like a real piece of work," he finally commented.

"At this point, I don't have much of a choice."

Carter agreed. "Why don't you go to the cops?" He thought it was a bad idea, but he needed to hear her reasons.

She glared at him. "Are you going to tell them? I already told you bringing in the police would get me killed."

"I'm not going to tell them, and I agree it might not be the best idea, but I wanted to hear your logic behind the choice."

She leaned back deeper into the couch and tucked her legs beneath her. "Because I think they, the cops, will make me keep going regardless. It would give them someone on the inside. And then, I lose control. Not that I have that much but if they are involved, I have to do whatever they say. I don't like that option. Also, Akela would definitely end up in prison and who knows what would happen to Kai. It's better to keep the cops out of it and deal with it myself. I make the money, pay Bobby off, and then we all go our separate ways."

Carter seriously doubted that was going to happen. There was no way a guy like Bobby was going to let a golden goose like Mia slip through his fingers. Not in this lifetime. Or any other. "Professional gambling. I gotta say, that was totally unexpected."

Mia lifted her chin. "I'm unexpected in all kinds of ways."

She could say that again. Carter was blown away by her and that in itself was a mystery to him. The gambling thing was just the icing on the cake.

"So what do you think? Still think you can help me?" Mia asked.

Carter nodded. "I can. I can keep you safe

while you're gambling and, once I get the lay of the land, maybe I can figure out a way to get Bobby off your back."

She shook her head. "Don't mess with Bobby. But if you can keep me safe until I get the money, that would be...helpful. I need to be able to concentrate totally when I play. I don't want Bobby or anyone else bugging me and I need to know that he's not going to just show up whenever he wants and catch me off guard." She shivered.

"Agreed. You should call him before he turns up here again. You need to arrange some sort of meeting location for whatever he wants. Tell him your place is off limits because your neighbors are already asking about him and you're pretty sure they'll call the cops if he shows up again. That should keep him away. I'll go with you to the meeting and make sure you're okay."

She nodded and picked up her cell phone. "You sure you're good with this?" she asked one more time as she dialed.

"More than sure."

"Okay then," she agreed.

"I'm just going to get my stuff and I'll be back shortly. Are you going to be okay here on your own or do you want to come with me?" Carter offered.

Mia looked up, the expression on her face totally confused. "Get your stuff? What are you talking about?"

"You can't stay here on your own. The threat of the cops will only keep him away for a bit. Either I move in here with you or you move out to my cabin at the ranch, which would be safer, but it's your choice." Carter did his best to keep the smile off his face but he had to admit he was looking forward to his new job. Maybe even a bit too much.

CHAPTER 11

MIA BIT her lip as she tried to stop her hands from shaking. Bobby's visit to her place earlier this morning had shaken her up more than she'd realized. Suddenly, she felt stupid for not telling Carter about the meet. She'd hired him after all, hadn't she? He was supposed to keep her safe. How could he do that if he didn't know where she was? She tried to do some breathing exercises to slow her heart rate down from stratospheric to merely a gallop.

Carter had just pissed her off so much with his moving in shit. Seriously. He'd just said Bobby probably wouldn't come back for a while so why did he have to move in? Or worse, have her move out to the ranch. No way in hell that was going to fly. Then everyone would know there was a problem. The Big Island was, in fact, a very small place, and nothing circulated faster than a juicy piece of gossip. No way she could go stay at the ranch without the world knowing. They'd either assume she was in trouble, which she was, or assume she was sleeping around, which she wasn't. But who would believe that after one look at Carter?

Not that she cared what people thought when it came to her sleeping around, but she did care when it came to her reputation. She'd built the business from scratch, and she was proud of it. The fact that her parents had been so damn proud of her because of her success meant she'd do anything to avoid doing something that might disappoint them. It didn't matter that they were dead. She would not bring shame to her family name. They would hate the fact that she was gambling again. Absolutely hate it. But they also would understand because she was helping protect her business and she was helping a friend in need. They'd always liked Akela and thought her upbringing had been a bit tough. They would want Mia to help in any way she could.

Now that she'd justified what she was doing by blaming dead people, she needed to haul her ass out of the car. Somehow her legs just wouldn't move. She stared out the windscreen into the darkness. The sound of waves hitting the shore filtered through, and usually she found it relaxing. Tonight, the sound was more ominous, nearly violent. The fact that Bobby wanted to meet at Honoli'i had seemed like a great idea earlier when she'd talked to him. She'd always loved this beach. It was one of her favorite surfing spots when she was a kid. This time of night, it just seemed desolate and scary.

The clouds parted and the moon shone through. The beach appeared empty and there were no other cars in the parking lot. Bobby had set this beach as their meeting place, so where the hell was he?

Over the dull roar of the crashing waves, the sound of an engine reached her, followed by a set of headlights in the rearview mirror blinded her.

Bobby's van had entered the parking lot. As it pulled up beside her she noticed Mele, known as Mikey, in the passenger seat, and Nakoa driving. They were two of Bobby's sidekicks from back in the day. They weren't too swift, if she remembered correctly, but they'd always been nice to her, or at least as nice as Bobby would let them be.

She took a deep breath. *Here goes nothing.* Mia opened her door and got out.

The van's side door opened. "Do you have the money?" Bobby snarled. He was sitting in the seat behind the passenger seat.

Mia was taken aback. How the hell did he know she'd made money? "Er, yes but not on me."

"Then what the fuck are we here for? I want that money." Bobby's lips were curled into a snarl. Despite the van's overhead light being dim, Mia noticed Bobby had a cut above his eye, and a thin trickle of blood dribbled down his face. *So that's why he was late.* Things did not seem to be going well for him.

"I'm not giving you the money until I have all of it."

She jumped back as Bobby shot out of the van. "That's not how this works, bitch! You do what I say, and I say give me the fucking money you won."

"That doesn't make sense," Mia stammered.

Bobby got right in her face. "You do what the fuck I say!"

She smelled sweat and bad breath and something else. The acrid tang of fear soured the air around her.

Bobby was afraid. *Well, he could join the fucking club.* She held up her palm in a *be reasonable* gesture. "I need money to gamble. If you want me to make two hundred and fifty grand in a couple of weeks, I need money to bet. I can't earn that kind of cash betting small. Nickel and dime betting means it will take months to hit your goal. I need to keep the money I won as my stake."

"She speaks the truth," a voice said from the back of the van.

Mia's head jerked up as she tried to look over Bobby's shoulder to see who was there. Panic hit between her shoulder blades. She'd been so focused on Bobby that she hadn't noticed anyone else in the back of the van. *Shit. Big mistake.* One Carter wouldn't make.

Suddenly, a shape blocked out the van light. The man got out and came to stand beside Bobby. "Hello, Mia. How have you been?" He ran his gaze over her body and then said with a smirk, "You're looking well."

Donny fucking Nakamura. Bile rose and she struggled not to wretch. "Donny." She acknowledged the other man but said no more. Donny gave her the creeps in a way Bobby never did. Bobby was a lowlife drug dealer with more issues than she could count. But Donny was an altogether different animal. He made her skin crawl, and after the look he'd given her, she wanted nothing more than to go home and take a shower. *Yuck.*

She turned back to Bobby. "I need money to make money. You can't expect me to gamble with no money."

Donny inclined his head. "She is, of course, correct, Bobby. She needs a decent amount of seed money if this little venture is to work."

Bobby frowned at Donny. "Stay out of this," he growled.

Donny ignored Bobby and continued, "Now, though, she knows that we know exactly how much she makes and she can start making payments at the end of the week. That will give her enough time to establish herself with Peter and use the ten grand to win bigger."

Bobby snarled at Donny and then turned a fierce glare toward Mia. "Fine, but I want to see you back here on Sunday night," he said and then started jabbing her in the shoulder as he contin-ued, "and you better be bringing me a lot of fucking cash or you and your friends are dead."

Mia's mouth was so dry she couldn't speak. She merely nodded her head.

"Lovely to see you," Donny said and then disappeared into the deep recesses of the van.

Bobby poked her once more. "Sunday fucking night and you had better bring me a lot of fucking money."

With a final glare, he climbed into the van. The driver threw the gear into reverse and was already backing up before Bobby even had the door closed. They were gone in seconds, leaving Mia to be pelted with the sand they'd stirred up.

Nearly hyperventilating, she slid down the side of her car, her head and neck jarring when her butt hit the ground. Why the fuck had she agreed to this? Carter was right; she was in way over her head. She hadn't been this out of sorts since the first time she'd been ragdolled under a massive wave. All that water pounding over her, tossing her about, had been terrifying. Similar to what she was feeling right this minute.

Mia's hands shook as she put them over her face. She needed a way out. She should call Emery and confess the whole story. Get Bobby and Donny arrested. If only. With the minimal information she had they weren't going anywhere. Who knew, she might be in a worse spot if the cops wanted her to stay in. Not to mention, Akela would have to testify and there was no way she was going to do that if Kai's life was threatened.

Going to the cops was a non-starter. She wouldn't do that until her back was to a wall embedded with nails poking into her.

Staring out at the ocean, she realized how right Carter had been. She couldn't handle this herself. Not with these assholes. Mia needed help.

She needed Carter.

The thought of him moving in, which had been an anathema to her twenty minutes ago, was the only thing that made her feel better after her encounter with Bobby and—she shivered—Donny. She wanted Carter with her twenty-four-seven. She was going to need his protection if she was going to make it through this. Hell, she wanted him with her at that moment, and suddenly, the shower she wanted to take didn't seem safe unless he was going to be in the house with her.

Yeah, she was well and truly screwed. She flexed her shaking fingers and pulled her phone out of her back pocket. Time to face the music. She glanced at the screen. Carter had called three times already. She might not know the guy well, but she knew him enough to know just how pissed he was going to be when she told him what she'd done. It wasn't going to be pretty, but his anger was nothing compared to the rampant fear the meeting with Bobby and Donny had instilled in her. She was willing to take the dressing down as long as Carter was still willing to protect her. It was suddenly crystal clear to her that the likelihood of her surviving this without his help was zero.

She hit the button on her phone screen.

"Carter?" she said when he answered.

"Mia, where are you? I thought we were going to meet at your place?"

"About that, I..." her voice gave out on her.

"Where are you? Are you okay? Tell me the address and I'll come to you." Concern laced his voice, and it was enough to clog her throat closed with unshed tears.

She swallowed hard and then cleared her throat. "I'm okay. I'm heading home. I'll be there in a bit, and I'll explain everything." She paused then added, "You were right. I can't do this on my own. Are you sure you still want to protect me? Because I think it's going to be a much tougher job than maybe you first thought. Things are worse than I realized."

"Mia, I'm in this. I promised I'd take care of

you. We made a deal. I'm going to stick by it no matter what the situation is. You have my word."

Relief bobbed through her, like sitting on a longboard in calm water. Breath came a little easier now. "I'll be at my place in about twenty minutes. Wait, are you hungry? I can pick up something on the way."

"Already done. Me and the food will be waiting. See you soon."

Mia clicked off the call and stared at the phone. Damn. She was so fucking lucky that she'd met this guy right when she needed him. Maybe the universe was taking care of her, or maybe, as she preferred to believe, her parents had put him in her path. Either way, she wasn't looking a gift horse in the mouth. She made sure to send up a prayer of thanks to both the universe and her parents and got back in her car. It was only going to get uglier from here, and she didn't want to piss any of the gods off.

She was going to need all the help she could get.

CHAPTER 12

CARTER GLANCED at Mia before he started pulling out the surveillance equipment he'd brought. Color was slowly returning to her cheeks and her hands seemed steadier than they'd been an hour earlier when she'd walked in the door.

He'd waited outside until it started to rain and then he'd picked the lock on her front door, mostly to see if it was as unsecure as he thought it was. He'd been right and was glad he'd stopped at a hardware store to purchase a new one. He'd fully expected her to yell at him for doing it when she'd arrived but instead, she just came in and collapsed on the stool at the kitchen counter. Clue number one about how badly shaken she was. The fact that her hands quivered like leaves in the wind, and her face was chalk white had been the giveaway. Whatever had happened, it had been unexpected and explosive.

And that pissed him off like nothing else.

"Mia," he called softly.

She opened her eyes. She'd been dozing on the couch. "Sorry. Just super tired. I need to take a shower and then get in bed. I was up all last night, and I actually worked today, so I'm running on fumes."

Carter nodded. "Go take your shower. I'm going to install some outdoor cameras after I finish changing your locks. I'll try to keep the noise down."

"Thanks." She didn't move.

"Mia?" He was concerned about her. She looked better but she wasn't bouncing back the way he'd thought she should.

"Sorry," she said again. "I'm just a bit…"

"Scared?" he offered.

She turned to look at him and nodded. "Yes. I guess that's the word. Donny Nakamura freaks me out. I wasn't expecting him. He's…a creep in all the worst sense of the word. The way he looked at me earlier made my skin crawl. Now, I just want to vomit. The idea of taking a shower…"

"You don't want to be vulnerable. You're

afraid to relax just in case something bad happens."

"Yes," she agreed. "How do you do it? How do you learn to relax after…"

He blew out a breath as he tightened the last screw on the new lock. "You're asking the hard questions." He straightened. "It takes training, honestly. Trusting my instincts to tell me if there's a problem. Trusting the people around me to have my back." That had been in shorter supply lately and he'd been suffering for it. He hadn't been sleeping well for weeks, so it seemed kind of hypocritical to be telling Mia she needed to relax. Gotta practice what he preached. "Look, it's not easy, but you will learn to adapt. My hope is this won't go on long enough that you'll have to learn all that. For right now, I'm here, asking you to trust that I will keep you safe. Donny will not get you while you're in the shower. I promise."

She bit her lip but nodded and then slowly got off the couch. "Thanks," she mumbled, then trudged down the hallway like she had lead weights wrapped around her ankles.

Carter watched her go and then lined up his equipment to install the cameras.

He gave her five minutes, then he walked down the hallway to the bathroom.

She was just coming out of her room to go in. "Oh sorry, do you need it?"

He shook his head. "No, I'm just checking it for you." He glanced in. It had been decorated in white and grey, sleek white tiles with streaks of gray in them. The shower stall was glass and there was nowhere else to hide. "It's all clear."

Was it necessary to announce the fact? Not at all, but he thought it might make her feel better. He walked down to the end of the bath and examined the window there. It was about two feet wide and maybe two and a half feet tall, but the window would only open to about eighteen inches. It was an odd size window, and the lock on it was crap, but he was certain no one was going to be able to climb through it without her being aware.

He turned towards her. "No one is coming in there without you seeing them, okay?" He pointed to the frame. "I can put up a stopper if you want so the window can't open more than a couple inches. It'll only take me a couple of minutes. Would you like that?"

Mia glanced at the window and then back at

him. "But then I can't get out if there's a problem."

"That's the downside," he agreed.

"Just leave it. I'm sure I will notice if anyone tries to get in that way." She paused, then asked, "Can you install a better lock on it, or an alarm so we'll hear if anyone tries to come in that way?"

"Sure. Not a problem." Carter closed the thick gray curtains. "You should be fine in the shower. If you want to leave the door open so I can hear you better, go for it. I promise not to look." He offered her a grin.

She laughed. "It's fine but thanks."

He nodded and left the bathroom. She was coming around, but it was going to be a long couple of weeks if she was this freaked out already. The reality of the situation was sinking in, and he didn't like the effect it was having. Mia was buckling under the weight. Hopefully, a good night's sleep, and having him there, would help her rally. All of this made him want to snap Bobby's neck. He hated the fact that Bobby and his cohorts were terrorizing Mia and her friend. There had to be more that he could do, but first, he needed to get the lay of the land. No, first he needed to secure Mia's house. Everything else would take time and planning.

Three hours later, Carter came in from installing half a dozen cameras outside. He walked down the hallway to Mia's room. The door was open a crack. He moved it slightly to check on her. She was fast asleep. That was good.

He moved back down the short hallway to his room, which was at the front of the house. He hated that Mia's room was on the opposite side, but the cameras he'd installed were operational, the software had been set to notify him. If anything bigger than a squirrel went by outside, his phone should alert him. That was going to have to be good enough.

He took a quick shower and then crawled into bed. He set his alarm for six a.m. and tried to relax. He hadn't heard from Castle but he hadn't expected to. Carter did some breathing exercises and then drifted off to sleep.

The sound of voices woke him. He glanced at his phone. Three a.m. He listened. Definitely two voices. His pulse quickened. He checked the camera app on his phone. Nothing. No one had entered the house. So where were the voices coming from? He got out of bed, grabbed his gun off the nightstand, and went into the hallway. The voices were coming from Mia's room. He quickly checked the rest of the house and then came back. Slowly he pushed open the door. Mia was sitting up in bed watching her iPad.

He put his gun down by his side as she looked up at him. "Sorry, I couldn't sleep." She looked guilty. "I didn't mean to wake you."

"Not a problem," Carter replied as he glanced around the room. The bed was huge and filled with pillows. She looked so small among them. "You get any sleep?"

"Yeah, but that's the problem with staying up all night. It screws with my sleep clock. I'll be up for hours now and then fall asleep in the morning."

Carter sighed. That meant he was going to be up for the rest of the night too. "Is there anything I can get you?"

She frowned. "Is there any pizza left? I'm hungry."

"Yeah, you want me to heat it up for you?"

"No, I've got it," Mia said as she got out of bed.

Carter's eyes bulged a little as he checked her out. The skimpy black tank top and a pair of sleep shorts clung to her. She was not wearing a bra, which made his mouth water. Yeah, that wasn't good. With her sleep-tousled hair, her friggin' sexy appearance had a direct line to his dick.

He moved out of the doorway to let her by. Her scent circled him as she passed by. Something citrusy with some kind of a flower. He ran a hand over the back of his neck, watching her hips as she walked away from him. He'd set night lights around the house to provide a dim light. The one in the hallway showed off how the sleep shorts clung to her ass. Carter decided then and there, he'd better go put some jeans on because he was starting to get hard, and she'd know right away if he stayed in his underwear.

After pulling on his jeans, he made his way out to the kitchen. Mia glanced up at him. She'd only turned on the light over the stove where she was heating up a couple of slices of pizza in a frying pan.

"I thought you might like a slice," she said as she gave him a quick smile. Her eyes lingered on his chest and her cheeks colored as she went back to staring at the pizza.

At least he wasn't the only one affected. It made him smile as he leaned against the counter. "I'm always up for pizza." He was up for all kinds of things at the moment and so was his cock, but he'd take pizza if that's all she was offering.

Desperate for a topic to relieve the tension, he decided now was as good a time as any to discover more about the sexy woman standing in front of him. "How did you discover you were good at blackjack?" he asked. Maybe talking about gambling would take his mind off how much he wanted to pull her to him and run his hands over her body.

"I used to surf." She glanced over at him. "I mean professionally. I was a serious professional surfer until I caught a bad wave and it collapsed on me, blowing out my knee. It was a freak thing but that was the end of my surfing career. Akela was surfing then too. We were close. She continued surfing, and I suddenly had nothing to do. No competitions to train for. After years and years of practicing every day, there was nothing to drive me forward. Up at four a.m., out on the water until six-thirty and then back home and off to school, or to the gym, or to see my coach. Suddenly, I had all this free time and I rapidly sunk into a weird depression. It's like if you drank an entire pot of coffee and then had to sit in a chair and not move." She shook her head.

"Anyway, someone was having a party and Bobby was there. He had a game going. I started playing. It was poker, and that's not really my thing but I did well enough that Bobby invited me to one of his backroom games. Eventually, I found blackjack and that was the end. I had found my next obsession. I could focus on playing like I did in surfing, and the high the game gave me was the same kind... I don't know...euphoria as I got from competitions. And of course, I won. A lot. I have a great memory."

"You count cards?" Carter blurted out. He could've kicked himself. He didn't mean to interrupt her. Mia obviously wanted to talk, and he loved hearing about her life. He was just so surprised. Card counting was hard, and it would get anyone kicked out of any casino. Management took that shit very seriously.

Mia tilted her head. "Not so much count and just remember what's been played and what hasn't. Then it's a matter of odds. I've always been good with numbers, and I bet conservatively." She shrugged. "It was fun. Too much fun."

"Too much?"

She checked the pizza. "Not quite ready." Turning back toward him, she sighed. "I started going to one of Bobby's games almost every night. I ended up sleeping all day and never seeing any friends. I blew off my parents on a regular basis and didn't bother to look for a job.

As far as I was concerned, I had one. I was a professional gambler and that was what I was going to do for the rest of my life."

Her face filled with sadness.

Carter touched her arm. "What happened?"

She sniffed. "My parents…" She stopped and cleared her throat and then started again. "My parents sat me down for an old-fashioned intervention. They stood me in front of the mirror and told me to take a good look at myself. For the first time in months, I did. I was shocked by what I saw. Who was that sallow-looking woman staring back at me? Exhaustion hung on me like a cloak. I'd always been lean, but I'd lost a lot of weight. My clothes seemed to be two sizes too big. All my muscle from surfing and working out was gone. I was a shadow of my former self."

She checked the pizza again and shook her head. "I suddenly could see and understand what they'd been telling me for months. I was out of control and if I didn't stop it would probably eventually make me super sick or kill me. So, I went to therapy, and went back to school. Since I was so good with numbers I studied accounting. I used the money I'd won in contests and from gambling to start my own accounting business. Things were going well and I had a life again."

She still looked sad and Carter braced for what was coming. He gripped the counter to stop from hugging her. He wanted to offer comfort and he wasn't sure she'd appreciate that. Mia was proud and strong. He found that aspect of her insanely appealing, but it also made things a bit sticky when it came to offering her any kind of help or support.

"A couple of years ago, my parents were killed in a car accident." She frowned. "It's been tough since then, but I've been managing. I'd promised them I wouldn't gamble ever again so this…situation is hard. Really hard."

The hell with this. Carter let go of the counter and immediately pulled her into his arms. "Mia, I am so sorry about your parents. About everything," he said as he wrapped his arms around her.

"Thanks. I don't think I really realized how tough this has been." She wrapped her arms around his waist and rested her cheek on his chest. "It's hard being on my own and this whole situation is just…crazy. I guess I've been running on adrenaline."

He kissed the top of her head. She looked up at him. He smiled. "You're not alone anymore. I'll help you get through this. I'm sure your parents would understand you gambling again to help your friends."

She nodded and her gaze locked with his.

Electricity speared straight to his groin. Before he could think about it, he leaned down and kissed her. Her lips were soft and inviting. They opened under his and he slipped his tongue into her mouth. She wrapped her arms around his neck and deepened the kiss. Her breasts were crushed against his chest, and he dropped his hands to her ass and brought her against his hard-on. She rubbed her pelvis against him and a moan escaped her lips.

Suddenly, a loud siren blared through the night. The smoke alarm was going off, and the pizza was billowing clouds of smoke on the stove.

"Shit," Mia said turning off the burner and coving the frying pan.

Carter grabbed a dish towel and waved it in front of the fire alarm. It took a moment, but it finally stopped screaming. He met Mia's gaze and the two of them burst into laughter. "So much for pizza," he said finally.

"Yeah."

"Wait, that doesn't go directly to any fire station or anything does it?"

She shook her head. "Nah, I burn food way too much to have that kind of systems. The fire department would be here all the time."

He grinned. "If you're still hungry, I can fix you something."

She shook her head. "No, I think I'm good. I'm just going to go back to bed." She started out of the kitchen and then turned back. "Carter?" she said. "Thanks for listening." She gave him a small smile and then turned and headed for her room.

He wanted to say something, to respond, but those words and that smile had left him speechless. If he wasn't careful, this job was going to rob not only his ability to speak but his heart as well.

CHAPTER 13

MIA TOOK a deep breath and let it out. She knew she had to bet more, but Peter still hadn't put her at her own table, and it was too much to gamble based on those around her. There was a new drunk guy tonight, Tony, and he was making all the wrong calls. It was killing everyone else's chances. He was using up cards that should've gone to the woman on her left. The woman, Mitzy, a blonde in her sixties from the mainland, was getting upset and Mia couldn't blame her. Tony was screwing the deal up for the three other people at the table.

Mitzy raised her hand and called, "Peter," in a loud voice. The tall slim man turned and made a beeline toward her.

"Yes, Mitzy?"

She dropped her voice so low Mia couldn't make out the words. Peter seemed to listen intently and then shot a glance at Mia. His eyes narrowed but he nodded and then turned and walked away. He grabbed two of his guys and they began setting up a new table.

Mitzy turned to Mia. "You haven't been playing here very long but you've played somewhere."

"Um, I used to play a few years back and then gave it up for a while." She smiled. "What about you?"

Mitzy shrugged. "I've been playing a long time. I used to do it professionally, but I married a rich man and now I just do it for fun. We're over here vacationing and he's off to bed early because he gets up at the ass-crack of dawn to golf. The idea of whacking a tiny ball, then chasing after it seems futile." She shuddered. "I can't stand golf, so I gamble at night and then sleep late. We meet for lunch. Works for both of us."

Mia wasn't sure what she was supposed to say to that information, so she just smiled. It was her turn. The dealer, the same Patty from the other night—although Mia suspected wasn't her real name since she was definitely of Hawaiian descent—dealt her a card face down and a nine of spades up.

Mia looked at her hole card. A seven of hearts. Sixteen. The dealer showed the ten of hearts and, of course, her own face-down card. Mia placed a bet and then tapped the table.

The dealer dealt her an ace.

Mia considered what her odds were and then placed another bet and tapped the table once more.

Again, the dealer gave her another card, this time the three of clubs. Twenty.

All the aces were showing, so Mia knew there was no point in continuing to take cards. She shook her head, and the dealer dealt to herself. It was the seven of clubs. The dealer promptly turned over her card to show that she'd had the five of spades.

Twenty-two.

Mia won. Relief washed over her like a rolling wave. She'd bet more than she'd felt comfortable with on that round. The risky move worked in her favor this time, but it wouldn't necessarily work out if she kept having to play at the table with Tony and the others.

Peter made eye contact and strode purposefully toward her. Mia's heart started to pound.

Was it illegal to memorize the cards played? The whole damn thing was illegal but was it cheating? Would Peter kick her out for cheating? That would be disastrous. She had no other way to raise the money in time.

Before he got too close, Carter stepped in between them. Peter came to an abrupt halt and looked confused. "Who are you?"

"I'm with Mia," Carter said. "Is there something you need?"

Mia's heart filled with gratitude for Carter's presence. She let out a pent-up breath. No matter what, he would help her. He would make sure no one hurt her.

"We've set up a separate table for Mia." Peter pointed to the table the men had just set up in the corner. A male dealer stood behind it.

"Sugar, you're too good to sit at this table," Mitzy stated. "So am I, but I don't care anymore. You do." She winked.

Mia placed a hand on Mitzy's arm. "Thank you," she said. "You have no idea how much I appreciate this."

Mitzy shrugged. "You look stressed. I have a feeling you've got a lot riding on all this. Good luck."

"Thanks," Mia said as she gave the other woman's arm a squeeze.

She collected her chips, tossed one to Patty as a tip, and then rose from her chair.

Carter escorted her, with a hand tucked against the small of her back, across the room to her new table. She sat down and he moved to stand against the wall. After giving her an encouraging smile, his eyes went back to scanning the room. Stress melted away from Mia's body, like a wave rolling out at low tide. Even though she was still in a bind, her chances had increased for her to get out of this whole mess in one piece.

Peter hovered at her elbow. "Mitzy seems to think you're good enough to deserve this table. I trust Mitzy, so we'll give this a try. But if you don't do well, or you try to screw me in any way, I'll shut you down." He gave her a 'we're watching you' kind of look.

Carter suddenly appeared next to Peter. "Please step back," he said, his voice cold and menacing. Peter stared at him for a long moment as his own security started to move in, but Peter waved them off.

"Is there anything I can get you Mia?" he asked.

"A Pepsi would be good."

Peter nodded but his gaze hadn't moved from Carter. "Don't push your luck," was all he said.

Carter's stare bored into Peter's back as the man walked away and signaled to one of his wait staff.

"You okay?" Carter asked.

Mia nodded. Her mouth had gone dry as soon as Peter had threatened her. She just needed to play the damn cards and get the hell out of here.

The dealer, Joe, smiled at her. "Are you ready?" He tapped the tabletop.

Mia nodded and he started dealing. It was going to be a long night if she couldn't get into the zone. She glanced at her chips and calculated that she was up about five thousand. At a minimum, she needed to triple that if she was going to get the money in time. *But hey, no pressure.* She surreptitiously wiped her hands on her dress and then checked her cards. *Here we go.*

CARTER LEANED against the wall and watched the crowd. There were a few wealthy people present, but mostly the tables were occupied by average people, getting dressed up for the opportunity to give their money away, as he saw it. The wealthy were allowed to pick any table and play and if they showed any talent whatsoever, they were taken to a high roller table. Honestly, Carter was surprised Peter didn't just sit them down at the high-roller table to begin with, but he supposed if they really sucked others would get angry.

Peter was an enigma. He was dressed in an expensive suit, but if Carter had to guess, he would say Peter came up hard. The man exhibited street smarts and above-average survival instincts. In any fight, he'd be the one to watch.

The rest of the security staff were a mix of general thugs and gym rats. No one really stood out as a threat. However, Carter didn't need to see the bulges in their waistbands to know they were all carrying. Still, when push came to shove, there were too many of them for Carter to take them all on and win. In a fair fight, he'd hold his own, But with this crowd, the odds were stacked against him. He might have to call in his buddies if this looked like it might turn ugly.

The dealer pushed a pile of chips in Mia's direction, but she didn't even acknowledge it. It appeared that she'd blocked everything out and settled into a zone to play once she was moved to her own table. Carter knew it was going to be a long night, but he was up for it.

At least doing something, even if it was mostly standing around and assessing the crowd, took his mind off Castle.

A sudden shout brought all activity in the room to a crashing halt. Mia immediately whipped her head in the direction of the noise. Carter quickly identified the source of the racket as the drunk who'd sat next to Mitzi at the other table. He moved to Mia's side and put a hand on her shoulder.

"It's okay," he said quietly. "They're just throwing out a drunk guy." Her shoulder relaxed under his touch,

The dealer asked if she wanted another card and Mia nodded. Carter returned to his post, but he could see the shout had wrecked her concentration. She made small bets for the next few hands but didn't manage to win again.

"Mia," he said as he approached her, "why don't we take a quick break? Go outside for some fresh air?"

She met his gaze, and the glazed look in her eyes told him he'd made the right decision.

She nodded, and as she stood, Peter arrived at the table. "Finished for the night?" he inquired.

"No," Mia shook her head. "Just taking a small break to use the restroom and get some air. I'll be back in ten minutes. Can you have someone watch my chips?" She looked up at him. "I know exactly how much I have on that table. I expect it to be the same when I get back."

It was Peter's turn to nod. "Of course. We'll look after it for you. Can I get you anything from the bar?"

"Another Pepsi please." Mia moved around Peter and headed in the women's bathroom. She was back out a few minutes later and Carter escorted her outside.

"How are you feeling?" He took a quick recon of the parking lot and didn't see anything alarming. There were a couple security guys stationed at the corner of the building and he was guessing a few more back by the street. He wasn't sure whose operation this was, but they were smart to have stationed security in spots where they could sound an early warning system in case the cops, or any other trouble, showed up.

Mia leaned against the wall. "I'm tired and hyper all at the same time." She rubbed her face. "I was making progress until that guy yelled. It really rattled me. Damn Bobby. If he and Donny hadn't freaked me out so much, this would be easier. Every loud sound or sudden movement has me jumping."

"I know. If it makes you feel any better, you will always be fine inside. Peter would do anything to avoid any kind of a scene. He sure as hell won't do anything to scare people off. Throwing out a drunk now and again is probably as bad as it gets. If he has an issue with you, he will wait until the room is empty or take you somewhere else."

She gave a snort. "Not as reassuring as you seem to think."

Carter grinned. "Call me an optimist. Seriously, if there's going to be a problem, it won't be here."

Mia bit her lip but then nodded. "That actually does make me feel better." She let out a long breath. "Okay let's go back in. I need to make a lot more money if I'm going to get what Bobby needs in time."

Carter held the door for her, and they went back inside. Mia went back to her table and sat down. "Good luck," Carter said and kissed the top of her head.

He went back to his post by the wall. Peter arrived with a can of unopened Pepsi. Carter had explained to him earlier that Mia wouldn't drink anything that could be tampered with. The other man had appeared somewhat affronted but just gave a curt nod. His job was to do what the clients wanted, no matter how insulted he felt.

The real question on Carter's mind was who was really running this place? It wasn't Peter. He was just a middleman who answered to someone else. There was a kingpin, but Carter didn't know enough about crime on the Big Island to have any idea who that might be.

Another hour went by. People gambled and mostly lost, as far as Carter could tell. There were a few winners, but Mia was by far the biggest. Now that she was more relaxed, it seemed to be easier to win.

A ripple of excitement went through the crowd. Carter scanned the room to see what had caused the reaction. Over by a side door, a group of six men entered. Security for someone. They were dressed in suits, and unlike the guys here at the warehouse, these men knew what they were doing. Their tattoos marked them as gang members, but Carter would bet good money that they had military experience as well. The military had a gang problem these days, and these men were part of the reason why. Go in as thugs and come out as killing machines with all the best skills and knowledge.

Carter studied the people the security staff appeared to be protecting. A tall man with a medium build. His black hair was cut in a stylish manner, and his suit was expensive. He was also vaguely familiar. It took Carter a minute but then it clicked. Mark Bascom. Head of Blue River Security, a security company that operated out of D.C. He'd made a name for himself in Iraq and now he ran with the big dogs. Several of Carter's retired friends had gone to work for Bascom. They liked the money but not one of them liked Bascom. Said he was all kinds of shady.

The man beside him was shorter and wider but tattoos peeked from beneath his collar. His suit was also expensive and there was no doubt he was wealthy by the flashy display of large gold and diamond rings on his fingers.

Peter greeted the newcomers, and by the way he moved, Carter surmised that the shorter man was Peter's boss. *So this was the man Bobby wanted to replace. No way in hell.* Bobby was penny ante and didn't have the balls to take anything from this man. And even if he did, Bobby would need a hell of a lot more than two hundred and fifty K.

Carter's gut tightened. This was not good news for Mia. Bobby was playing out of his league, and the sinking realization in his gut affirmed that it was going to come back to bite Mia.

Carter glanced at her as he scanned the room and focused once more on the two new visitors. Mia was totally in the zone and doing well. Blissfully unaware was a good thing. He needed her to stay relaxed because he was starting to tense up. This situation had just turned way more dangerous than Carter had bargained for. Dealing with Bobby was a pain in the ass. Dealing with Bascom and whoever this man was, yeah that was a whole other league. Mia needed to keep flying under the radar. Keeping her as just another decent player was the best approach.

Just as Carter had that thought, Mia won again. And it must have been a huge win. The amount of chips the dealer was pushing in her direction was mind-boggling. The dealer signaled a runner and whispered something to the lanky kid in the too-big suit. The kid sprinted across the floor toward Peter. Carter's spine tingled. This wasn't good. The kid whispered to Peter and then backed away. Peter looked over at Mia. Then Peter's boss said something to which Peter replied and pointed to Mia.

Carter's pulse ticked faster; like the red lights on a timer seemed to do as they approached zero right before something went boom! Peter and the two men started across the room toward Mia, who remained blissfully in the zone.

Fuck. Fuck. Fuck. Carter moved in beside Mia and let her finish her hand. He cupped her shoulder.

She glanced up at him, annoyance flashing on her face. "What?"

He gestured with his chin. She turned and the color drained from her face as the men stopped beside her.

The shorter man said, "How nice to see you again, Mia. It's been too long."

"H-hello," she said her voice quavering.

The man glanced over at Carter. "And who is this?"

He extended his hand as if he hadn't a care in the world. "Carter Nolan, Mia's boyfriend."

The other man raised his eyebrows. "Mia, you didn't mention you had a boyfriend. I expect to be kept abreast of all the big happenings in your life." He shook Carter's hand and tried to squeeze it, but Carter gave as good as he got and the man broke the tight clasp.

Carter nudged his hip into Mia's "Aren't you going to introduce me?"

Mia swallowed. "C-Carter," she said and then cleared her throat. "This is my uncle, Makaio Hale."

Carter kept his face bland while his heart about galloped out of his chest. Queasiness erupted once his stomach hit his knees.

The man Bobby wanted to replace was Mia's uncle?

Holy Shit! He hadn't seen this coming, not in any way, shape, or form. He glanced at Mia's white face. Carter needed to get her out of here and then she'd better start talking 'cause things just went sideways from where he was standing, and he wasn't sure if he could protect her anymore.

CHAPTER 14

Mɪᴀ's ʜᴀɴᴅ shook as she drank deeply from her wine glass before setting it down on her counter and facing Carter. "I know you must have a lot of questions, but I need a minute."

She hadn't seen her uncle in years. His popping up like...like some creepy clown in a horror movie freaked her out. Except, this wasn't a movie theater, and she couldn't get up and walk out.

Carter crossed his arms over his chest and leaned against the fridge. "I let you put me off during the entire ride back here. If you're trying to make up some kind of lie and it hasn't come to you yet, then another minute isn't going to help."

Mia's heart stuttered. His face was so serious,

as if he really believed she'd set him up somehow. "That's not fair."

"Really? Your uncle is the kingpin of the gambling world on the Big Island, and you didn't think to mention that to me? That's what I'd classify as not fair. I said I would help you with Bobby. Did you not tell me because you were afraid that I wouldn't help you if I knew about your uncle? Or is this all just some big setup to get me involved in this shit so you can screw with me?"

"If you remember, you insisted on helping me. I never asked. And I sure as hell wouldn't screw with you." Breathing hurt as Mia tried to get the words out. How the hell was she supposed to explain? How was she going to get him to believe her? She took another gulp of wine. "I'll tell you the whole thing just…just give me a minute." She ran shaking hands over her face. Since seeing him, her lungs had forgotten how to work, and each breath was a struggle. Running into her uncle had made her parents' deaths fresh.

"Look, Carter…" she licked her dry lips. "My uncle…I didn't know okay? I mean I knew he was bad news. He's been involved with organized crime forever. But I had no idea he had taken over the whole gambling thing. The last time I was involved, it was Bobby." She put a hand over her heart.

The muscle in Carter's jaw pulsed as he stared at her. "And you didn't think to give me the heads up that your uncle was a crime boss?"

Mia's stomach twisted into knots as she stared at her wine. Forget the glass, she wanted to down the bottle. "No, I didn't." She let out a long sigh. "He's my mother's brother. They had a falling out a long time ago. My mom always said that her brother was jealous of her relationship with their father. My grandfather apparently loved my mother more, or at least that was what everyone thought, including Uncle Makaio. That was… He was incensed about it."

She stood and started pacing, suddenly unable to sit still. "The only time he came to the house was when my grandfather was visiting. He would come, have tea or a meal and then leave again. It was awful. Full of tension that, even as a kid, I picked up on. Once my grandfather died, my uncle never came back.

"I didn't know anything about him being involved in organized crime until I started gambling. I had no idea about any of it until the day my parents staged an intervention. My mother told me then about Uncle Makaio, that he was involved in organized crime, and she was worried I would somehow get pulled into that life if I kept running with the gambling crowd. She was extremely upset and worried about it. Her story had the desired effect. I stopped immediately."

She turned and met Carter's gaze. "I truly had no idea he was behind the gambling scene, Carter. I haven't seen him in years. He didn't even attend my parents' funeral. I just blocked him from my mind. It never occurred to me that he was involved." She tapped her heart again. "I would have mentioned it. I swear I would've."

Carter's continued silence made Mia want to scream. "Look, if you want out, then just leave. You don't have to be involved in this. You never did. You insisted I needed your help. That's on you. If you're done, then just get out." She waved her arms toward the door. "I don't need this shit on top of everything else."

"I'm not leaving." Carter's voice was calm, cold even, and the pulse still jumped in his jaw.

Mia frowned and resumed pacing. "What do you want then? An apology? I'm sorry. I really am. I just...blocked out everything about my uncle. I met him a total of three times in my entire life before tonight. No one even knows we're related. My mother was always embarrassed by him, and he hated her, so it wasn't like they told anyone. They grew up on Oahu, meaning there weren't neighbors or relatives here to rat them out. I think that's why my parents moved here. My mother couldn't be far enough away from him. I had no idea he was here on the island even. I really just never thought about him."

"Okay," Carter said but he still looked pissed.

She stopped her pacing in front of him. "Okay? What the hell does that mean?" she demanded, hands on hips. "You believe me? You're done and you want to go? You've obviously still pissed off. Well guess what? So am I. This just made my life that much more complicated," she snarled

She was tired and pissed and freaking scared. The man who'd demanded to help her had suddenly turned frigid. What the fuck did he want?

She glared at him. "Just fucking go." She poked him in the chest with every word. "I don't need your attitude.

A smile tugged at the corners of Carter's lips suddenly.

"Are you laughing at me?" Mia demanded incredulously.

"You're awfully cute when you're pissed off."

She opened her mouth to tell him off when he swooped down and claimed her lips. He wrapped his arms around her and crushed her to his chest. She struggled to escape his embrace but clasped her arms around his neck instead. The kiss deepened and the heat of it ratchetted up as she pressed herself against him and rolled her hips. This felt so damn good. She was beyond caring about anything.

As he scooped her up, she wrapped her thighs around his waist. He carried her to the bedroom, laid her on the bed, and then covered her body with his own. Her hands caressed the hard ridges of his chest through his t-shirt, and fire coursed through her veins. He was rock hard, and she was desperate to have him inside her.

He pulled her dress up over her head and then tossed it on the floor. He pulled down her bra, exposing one breast for him to suckle. He devoured her nipple with his mouth as desire took complete control of them both.

"Carter," she breathed.

He planted soft kisses along the side of her neck. She let out a moan and grabbed his t-shirt.

Lifting on one hand, he pulled the garment off with the other, dropping it to the floor before he lowered his weight onto her once again. She reveled in it.

His lips searched hers while she traced circles around his back with her fingertips. He pulled back from her as she shivered beneath him.

"Are you cold?" he asked.

"Not at all," she replied breathlessly.

He unclasped her bra and pulled it free. When he brushed his tongue over one of her nipples she moaned. "God, that feels so incredible," she whispered.

She reached for his belt buckle, but he stopped her hands, grasping both of her wrists and holding them above her head. He took control of the kiss again, their tongues dancing with desire. Then he moved slowly down from her lips to her neck and then to each of her nipples, tugging lightly at them until she gasped for air.

She tried to free herself from his grip, but he held on tight. "Stop fighting and let me play." He nipped her breast and she yelped. He pulled away again and then rolled her onto her belly. Holding her hands above her head, he kissed her neck and pressed his hard-on against her backside.

His cock nestled against the seam of her ass was so damn hot. Heat coursed through her. She moaned his name.

He reached his hand around to find the apex of her legs and then massaged her through her thong.

"Get naked," she demanded and pushed her hips upward. Mia lifted her hips higher. Then he kissed her neck as he worked his fingers inside her thong. He rubbed her clit gently. She was wet with anticipation, pushing back and forth as his fingers moved at a leisurely pace.

"Faster," she ordered, and he increased his speed.

Under him, she writhed until he finally plunged his fingers inside of her, which elicited a yelp of pleasure from her lips.

He turned her over again and took off her underwear. She loved an alpha male streak when it came to sex. And he was as alpha as they came, making her want him desperately.

Carter pressed his body completely against hers, trapping her against the bed as he kissed her again. The touch of his skin against hers ignited an uncontrollable need. When he fingered the hot center between her legs, she moved fiercely trying to direct his attention inside her body. A sexy-as-sin chuckle told her he knew what she was trying to do, But he procrastinated, kissing her neck while flicking his fingers against her clit. He made his way down her body until he was kneeling on the floor, positioned above the apex of her legs.

He blew on her heated center while she dug her fingers into his scalp. His grip on her ass kept her still as he increased the intensity of his tongue. Then slowly, finally…mercifully, he eased one finger inside while continuing to swirl his tongue around her clit.

Her hands moved to caress his hair as she lifted her hips to meet his mouth. Tightening his fingers on her butt, he lifted her hips, and planted his mouth against her core, sucking and licking her to a frenzy. She got closer and closer to the edge until finally, he nipped her clitoris with his teeth, which triggered a jolt through her body.

His name slipped from her lips as she reached her climax.

"Carter, I want you inside me," Mia demanded. She wanted to feel him. To taste him. He started to kiss her, but she backed off. "Take off your jeans now." She helped him out of the rest of his clothing and then pushed him gently until he was lying on his back on the bed.

She straddled him then, determined to enjoy this time with him for as long as she could, she kissed him deeply, tasting her release on his lips and tongue. Then she traveled her lips down his neck to his chest. With her teeth, she teased his nipples, and he groaned. He tried to grab her ass, but she squirmed away from him.

"Mia." His low voice rumbled from his chest and spread shivers across her body.

She touched the hard planes of his abdomen, running her fingers over the tight, thick muscles. He was so damn beautiful. She wanted to burn his image into her memory.

She toyed with his nipples, licking and pinching, and then trailed lower to hover her mouth over his cock. She ran her tongue across the tip before making slow circles around the crown, first one way and then the other. Gradually, she drew him deeper into her mouth as she sucked and twisted. She kept her fingers tight around the base and cupped his balls with her other hand.

Carter growled her name; his deep voice creating shivers along her spine. She wanted him inside of her, but first, she yearned to hear him say her name again. His hips began to move, and she responded with her tongue.

"Mia, you're killing me."

She stopped and looked up, staring into his eyes as she ordered, "Don't come yet."

Then she smiled wickedly before returning to her previous position. The fact that he wanted her so badly made desire course through her body. She was already soaking wet with anticipation. When she started to ease herself over him, he grabbed her hips and pulled her down hard.

She gasped as she stretched to accommodate his girth. "You need to wait."

"Fuck waiting." He began moving his hips underneath her. She moaned and arched to take him in fully. She matched his rhythm and urged him to go faster.

"Jesus, Carter. You feel so damn good inside me. Faster," she demanded again. He obliged, holding her hips as she rode him.

"Mia," he said through gritted teeth. She knew he was on the verge of coming but so was she. She ground her clit over his pubic bone and keened as sensation roared through her. She arched, her hips bucking as she came. A few long, deep strokes later, he careened over the edge with her.

Exhausted, sated, but still wanting more, she flopped down onto his chest. Her body trembled from the intense, earth-shattering orgasm. But a hollow feeling was already building in her chest.

Her world was a mess and she was dragging this man down. She couldn't let him drown along with her. She wouldn't be responsible for him getting hurt, and with her uncle on the scene, the odds of someone not making it out alive were almost one hundred percent.

CHAPTER 15

CARTER GLANCED over at Mia as he made the turn into the industrial area. She hadn't said much since he picked her up. He'd left her place early on Monday morning without waking her. She'd been up most of the night gambling and then they spent the last few hours before dawn having amazing sex. He'd crashed for two hours and then slid out quietly to go to work. More equipment testing which was a complete waste of time, but he couldn't let his team down. Their orders were to test equipment so that's what they did. They had to run some night tests, so he didn't make it back to her until today.

"I'm sorry about Monday and Tuesday. We had to run night tests, and I needed to catch up on my reports." He smiled at her. "Not to mention my sleep. I did keep up with the cameras, though, and if Bobby or anyone had shown up, I would have been there ASAP."

She just nodded. "It's fine. The gaming doesn't run on Mondays and Tuesdays anyway. It usually doesn't run on Wednesdays either, but tonight's game is special. Peter called and invited me. It's a high-roller evening. Only the very good can play." She shrugged. "I guess I should celebrate that I've achieved high roller status, right? Woo hoo! Yay me." She turned and looked out the side window.

The guys had razzed him about Mia but he hadn't volunteered anything. Telling them her story felt like betraying her without getting her permission first, but he was determined to get it tonight. Her uncle and his apparent friend, Mark Bascom, had spun his world on its axis. Carter didn't want to have to take on those two men and their minions without his teammates.

"Mia, you're quiet. Are you okay?"

"Sorry. Just worried about my uncle. I don't want to run into him again." She played with the belt on her dress. This one was a deep purple sweater dress that clung to every curve. Carter couldn't wait to pull that belt free and watch it hit the floor. He'd been fantasizing about that very thing since he picked her up.

"Do you want to skip tonight?"

She sighed. "I don't think I can and still make the money for Bobby."

Carter made a left and steered toward the end of a parking lot. He pulled into a space in front of an auto body shop that was closed for the night.

"What are you doing?" Mia asked.

"Honey," Carter said as he turned towards her, "I don't think it's a good idea for you to go in there when you're like this. You need to concentrate to win."

Mia's shoulders drooped. "I know. I know. This whole situation is just so... I haven't really slept in the last couple of nights thinking about it."

Guilt hit him like a gut punch. "I'm so sorry I couldn't be there with you. I wanted to be." *Desperately.* The intensity of his desire shocked him, but he knew it to be true. There was just something about Mia that made him want to be with her all the time. To protect her with everything he had.

She gave him a shy smile. "I missed you. Not just because you make me feel safe, either.

Although you do. I didn't realize how alone I felt until you started coming around with all those meals. You've made a big difference in my life. Thanks for that." She leaned over and gave him a quick kiss. He held the back of her head and deepened it but then reluctantly broke it off a moment later.

"I'm sorry I'm not...focused. I just don't know what to do. If I keep going, then I am working for Bobby against my uncle. Not a huge deal in terms of him being family, but I have no idea what he would do if he found out. I'm so screwed. If I stop working for Bobby, he'll hurt Akela and Kai. If I go to my uncle and tell him about Bobby, then there's a solid chance he would have Bobby killed." She juggled her hands up and down, as if trying to weigh something out.

Carter sensed she was holding something back and his stomach tightened. "What is it, Mia?"

She stared at him for a moment then reached out and put her hand on his thigh. "I didn't tell you this not because I wanted to keep you in the dark but because I didn't think you'd believe me. No one believes me, not even my friends."

What did that mean? "Try me," he said trying to

keep his voice even. Sweat broke out between his shoulder blades. Any more surprises from Mia and he'd have to rethink things, and he wasn't sure he could do that. He braced for whatever she was about to say.

Mia licked her lips. "I've always thought that Bobby killed my parents."

Of all the things he thought she might say, that hadn't even crossed his mind. He covered her hand with his. "Why?"

"My parents were killed instantly when their car went off the road and crashed into the trees. The evening was clear. There were no other cars on the road. They'd been out to dinner, but my father was driving, and he didn't drink. The police could find no reason for them to have gone off the road, so they told me that my father likely swerved to avoid an animal and then lost control. The car was completely totaled, and they claimed there was too much damage for them to determine if anything had gone wrong mechanically, although I was told that was very unlikely."

Carter's heart ached for Mia. He couldn't imagine losing his parents that way. He wanted to pull her into his arms and hold her tight. Instead, he let her continue to tell her story.

"You're wondering why I think it had to do

with Bobby." She sighed. "He'd gone to prison for selling drugs but there was a rumor someone had ratted him out. He thought it was me for some reason and he'd threatened me. He'd just gotten out of prison a week before my parents were killed. I thought the timing was suspicious, so I asked a friend who's a cop to look into it. Emery came back with the same answers that the original investigating officers had.

"The thing is, I was supposed to be with them that night but I had a bad headache, so I stayed home. She glanced out the window before meeting his gaze again. "I know it sounds crazy, but my gut says that Bobby killed them. I think he was trying to kill me, and my parents just got in the way."

God, the guilt that must have caused her. Still haunted her. Carter gave up fighting the pull and hauled her into his arms then. "Mia, it's not your fault. Even if Bobby killed them, it's not on you. It's on him. Please don't blame yourself. The police were probably right, honey. Your dad swerved to avoid hitting an animal. It's instinct. But even if they were wrong, whatever happened, it's not on you."

Mia leaned into him. "Thanks. That's nice to

hear and kind of you to say but the guilt still torments me, you know?"

"I get it, honey. It's a heavy load to carry." He wanted to take her pain away, erase all her guilt. "Let's make a plan. Maybe there's some way to find out for sure about Bobby. Let me think on it but maybe we can get him to tell us the truth."

She pushed away from him. "You believe me?"

"I think it's possible. Let's think on it and see what we can devise to make Bobby tell the truth."

She smiled and then kissed him. This time she wrapped her arms around his neck and pressed herself against him. Carter kissed her back and was just contemplating if he should untie her dress when a sound reached his ears. He broke off the kiss.

"What is it?" Mia asked.

Carter frowned. "It's the rumble of a large diesel vehicle. That shouldn't be here at this time of night. It's not an eighteen-wheeler or anything like that." He knew the sound. It was similar to the rumble of a Humvee. Mia turned to look out the side window just as the first police vehicle turned the corner. It was followed by three more and then two armored police vehicles. That was what he'd heard. He'd know that sound anywhere. It was part of his job to recognize vehicles at night and in the dark.

"Holy shit! What the hell is going on?" Mia breathed as three more cop cars went past.

"Looks like your uncle's place is getting busted." Carter turned the SUV's engine over and backed up. He kept the headlights off.

"Where are we going?"

He glanced at Mia. "We're getting the hell out of here. Nothing good can come from staying." Two final police cars sped past. Carter turned right out of the parking lot. He didn't turn on his headlights until they were well away from the area. "We're going back to my place tonight."

Mia glanced at him. "Why do you think my place won't be safe?"

"Let's just say I don't want to take any chances."

He wasn't about to point out to her that she'd accepted the invitation to play but hadn't shown up. That would look suspicious to her uncle. Mia's life had just taken on a new level of danger and Carter didn't want to have to give her the bad news unless he absolutely had to. They'd stay at the ranch tonight and, if he had his way, every night thereafter. Mia's life could possibly be in danger, and he didn't want to find out if he was right.

CHAPTER 16

MIA GLANCED at her watch for the twentieth time pissed at the way this day was dragging on. Carter had left early this morning, after another round of amazing sex, then lying safe in his arms through the night. She smiled just thinking about it. How he managed to stay awake all day and go like a stud all night was beyond her. She'd fallen back to sleep after he left and had slept in until noon.

Although time had dragged, she'd kept busy all afternoon by dealing with some client work and making sure everyone's books were in good order. Nothing she could do about Akela's books at the moment. Even thinking about that mess gave her a headache.

Her cell rang and she glanced at the screen.

"Speak of the devil," she murmured. "Akela," she said by way of a greeting.

"Oh my God, Mia, I'm so glad you answered the phone! I just heard from Bobby that the gambling den at the industrial complex got busted last night. He thought you were there."

"I was running late. I hadn't made it there yet." She wasn't about to tell Akela that she'd been having a panic attack less than three blocks from the destination at the time of the bust. "What else did Bobby tell you?"

"He said that Peter had a high roller event going and they all got busted. He was practically crowing about it. According to him, the players who were there are super pissed at being arrested and dragged down to jail. Of course, some of them managed to talk their way, or bribe their way, out of it from what he said, but enough of them went down that Peter is in a tsunami of trouble. Bobby says the expectation is that Peter would've paid off the cops not to bust the place so the fact that the bust happened makes him look bad."

"Was the big boss there? The guy who runs it?" Mia's breath caught as she asked She cleared her throat. She couldn't even bring herself to say her uncle's name, not that Akela knew who Mia was truly related to.

"Apparently not, which Bobby was truly pissed about." Akela's voice changed. "I'm so glad you weren't there. I would feel just awful if you got busted over all this."

Me too. Mia drew in a deep breath. It had been a close call and she had to admit it scared the life out of her. "Did Bobby say anything else?"

Akela got quiet.

"What did he say, Akela?" Mia demanded.

Akela's voice got quiet. "Mia..."

Mia's stomach dropped at her friend's tone and dread filled her veins. "What?"

"Bobby said that if you called the cops and ratted Peter out to get out of this mess, then you were dead wrong about it. We still owe him and he expects to collect on time."

"He said that? He thought I ratted Peter out?" Mia's heart sped up, the way it used to when she was about to drop in on a massive wave. "Bobby thinks I'm the rat? Did he say if anyone else thinks that?"

"He didn't say. Why? Did you call the cops?" Akela demanded.

"No! I know just how stupid that would be." And

not just because of Bobby, but because of her uncle. Then it hit her. That's why Carter had her stay here at the cabin last night. He knew then that she might look like the rat, and he wanted to protect her. Her knees wobbled, gave way, and she collapsed onto the dining table chair. Staring sightlessly out the window, she suddenly realized she was in much deeper than she thought. She was upside down under a crashing surf and there was no way out.

"If it wasn't you, then you need to tell that to Bobby. He thinks it was you."

Shit. Shit. Shit. If he went around town saying that, then Peter and, worse, her uncle would hear it and assume that, despite his reputation as a lying sack of shit, Bobby was right. She'd be blacklisted from gambling, not a bad thing, but they might decide to take her out completely. Would her uncle do that? She couldn't imagine it. They weren't close but they were still family. Would he have his only niece killed?

"Mia?"

"Yeah, sorry. I'm just floored. I...I'm not sure what to do?"

Akela sighed. "I know what you mean." Silence stretched out, a lifetime between them, and then Akela asked, "How much money have you made? For Bobby, I mean."

"Sixty thousand."

"Wow. That's a lot. You must be really good."

Mia rubbed her forehead. "Yeah, I am. But it's not enough and now I have no way to make it for Bobby. Listen, I have to go. I'll keep in touch." She hung up without waiting for her friend to respond. She was kind of done with Akela today. Honestly, she wanted to blame the other woman for getting her into this mess, but at the same time, she knew she might have done the same thing if the situations were reversed. It was better to hang up before she said something she might regret.

Glancing at her watch yet again she made up her mind. It was only a little after five p.m. She could get out and go to Ohana's. Emery would be there soon and maybe she could find out from her friend who snitched on the gambling hall. She wasn't sure what she would do with the information, but a name in her back pocket would be a fantastic ace in the hole. She was starting to think she was going to have to go see her uncle and see if he could get her out of this mess.

Her mind briefly flicked to Carter. Although guilt rose up her spine, she couldn't wait for him. She'd welcomed him into this mess, but this was next level. He hadn't volunteered for this kind of danger. There was no way she wanted to risk his life. God, if anything happened to him because of her, the guilt would destroy her. She'd never recover.

Grabbing her purse, she made her way outside only to realize she didn't have her car there. "Shit." She pulled out her phone and booked a ride share. Then she hiked down to the gate and waited. Twenty minutes later, she climbed out of the rideshare in front of her house. She immediately got into her car and headed toward Ohana's. It wasn't until she was halfway there that it suddenly occurred to her that she hadn't left a note or anything for Carter. She gave a mental shrug. He'd text her and she'd get back to him then.

She pulled into Ohana's parking lot and looked around. The place was already filling up. It was almost six on a Friday night, so that was par for the course. Mia strolled inside and grabbed a stool at the scarred wooden bar.

"Hey, girl," Dahlia called. "You've been scarce lately. How are you?"

"Been busy. How are things?" She purposely didn't answer the other woman's question. *How was she? In a hell of a mess and trying not to fall apart.*

"What can I get you?" Dahlia asked as she washed some glasses.

"I've gotta drive."

Dahlia nodded. "A half glass of wine?"

"Sure. I could use a sip or two." Mia rolled her shoulders and tried to relax. She was among friends here at least. "Is Moana singing tonight?"

Dahlia shook her head. "Not tonight. We have some cover band in. I can't remember the name." She went off to get someone a drink and then came back. "I hear you've been spending some time with that cute guy, Carter."

Fire blew up her cheeks. "Yes." Her simple answer was belied by the smile lighting her face.

Dahlia grinned back and placed the half-filled glass of wine in front of her friend. "I like the smile on your face. It's been a while since I've seen it."

"Yeah, it's nice." She took a sip of wine and willed the heat away. "Is Emery around?"

Dahlia laughed and shook a finger. "Trying to change the subject? Fine, I'll let you get away with it this time but I want to hear details eventually."

"Deal." Mia let out a sigh of relief. She wasn't ready to talk about Carter just yet.

"Emery won't be in until much later. There was a big bust last night and she's working late."

Mia's throat went dry. "What kind of bust?" she asked trying to be casual. She wanted another sip of wine, but her hands were sweaty, and she was afraid she'd drop the glass.

"Gambling ring. In one of the warehouses over in the industrial complex. Be right back." Dahlia moved down the bar to pour more drinks.

Mia sat, breathing slowly as she tried for patience. She needed information but she wasn't sure it was the best idea to sit and wait for her friend. Emery was a good cop and Mia would have to play this close to the vest. Mia wasn't sure she could get the information she needed without showing her cards. She loved Emery but she still wasn't positive that telling her friend the whole story was a good idea, although it was looking less and less like she had any options.

Dahlia came back. "What was I saying? Oh right. About the bust. I heard some bigwigs got taken down. People like that aren't used to seeing their names in anything but the society columns."

"I'm sure it was a shock. How did it come about, did Emery say?"

Dahlia shrugged. "She didn't say but I got the impression they had a man on the inside."

Mia's heart thundered and her stomach pitched downward, the kind of roll a surfer might feel sliding into a trough. She battled the resulting nausea. If the cops had a man on the inside then they were bound to know Mia had been gambling. Worse yet, her uncle might think she was the inside person.

"You okay? You look like you've seen a ghost." Dahlia's face filled with concern.

Mia waved her off. "Sorry. Just been a long week." She stood. "You know what? I think I'm gonna head home. Take a bath, eat, and make an early night of it." She stepped onto the foot rail and leaned across the bar to give her friend a hug.

"Don't work so hard, Mia. Take care of yourself. Better yet, get Carter to take care of you." Dahlia grinned.

Mia gave her a halfhearted smile as she waved and then left. Before she pulled away from her parking space, she sent a text to Carter to let him know she was leaving Ohana's and heading to her place. She wanted to pick up some clothes.

The wrap dress had been fine for gambling and even working, but she wanted comfy clothes now and she really wanted a shower. She would throw some things in a bag and meet him back at the ranch.

The sun had set by the time she'd showered and gotten back on the road. She hadn't heard from Carter, but he'd said they might work late. Her stomach rumbled and she realized it was her turn to pick up dinner. She ran through a list of options in her head, then decided on Chinese. She stopped at her favorite spot and picked up a few different things, hoping Carter would like her choices. Then she was back on the road.

She was just outside of town on her way to the ranch when headlights popped up in her rearview mirror. The glare was blinding. The car behind her was running with high beams. It wasn't dark enough to warrant that yet. She tilted the mirror a bit and then glanced in the side mirror. The headlights were a lot closer.

"Someone's in a hurry," she murmured. She glanced down at the speedometer. She was slightly over the speed limit. The driver of that car could go around her if they were in that much of a hurry. She was not speeding up. She checked the rearview mirror again. The vehicle behind her looked like some sort of SUV, and it was way too close for comfort.

Dread thrummed in her chest. Was this Bobby, or Peter, or worse, one of her uncle's people? A shiver raced down her back, but she was determined not to panic. Panicking would only put her in more danger. Horror filled her at the thought that this was how her parents might have felt just before the crash.

The SUV behind her came closer still. Her sweaty palms slipped on the wheel as her gaze went from the road to her mirrors then back to the road again. It was wide open, and there were dotted lines coming up. Maybe they were just getting ready to pass? The dotted lines came and went. The SUV stayed behind her, mere inches from her bumper. She glanced over to the passenger seat, but her purse was too far away for her to reach her cell. God, how stupid could she have been? Carter warned her not to go out today, but she hadn't listened. Regret fought with fear as she glanced in her rear view mirror once again.

Suddenly her car jolted. Mia screamed as she gripped the wheel hard, trying to keep her vehicle on the road. The truck rammed her again, harder this time. Her seatbelt held her in place, but she jerked the wheel accidentally and veered out of her lane. Her heart thumped wildly in her chest as she tried to figure out what to do. The road was empty for miles, and she was climbing. If she went off the road, it was a long drop.

She looked in the mirror, but the SUV had dropped back. It was slowing down, and the headlights were getting smaller. Mia sagged with relief. Whoever it was had stopped. Maybe they'd realized they were playing a dangerous game. Or maybe they were just trying to scare her. *You were wildly successful.* Mia just wanted to get back to the ranch. Another glance in the rearview mirror revealed the lights were gone.

Mia slumped and eased her grip on the wheel and put her hand over her heart. Dear God, she did not need any more scares tonight. Just then, her cell went off and she jerked her shoulders. It had to be Carter trying to reach her. She would be at the ranch in ten minutes and she couldn't wait. She just wanted to spend the rest of the night with Carter. He made her feel safe and secure and sexy as hell. Sighing she thought about how she wanted to be in his arms right now.

Her car suddenly rocked forward. Mia's

scream filled the interior. She wrestled with the wheel to keep the vehicle on the road. The SUV was back, only this time the lights were off. She braced for a second hit. The SUV pulled around as if to pass her and hit her back tire dead center. Mia fought with the wheel, but the car turned sideways. The other driver hit the brights, and she was temporarily blinded as the SUV crashed into the side of her car again, pushing her. She looked out the passenger side window and saw... nothing. She was off the road with nothing but air around her.

Her tires lost their grip on the road, and the car vaulted over the guardrail. She screamed as she rolled over again and again. The cacophony of shattering glass and bending metal was deafening. It seemed to last forever. And then, sudden silence. Mia tried to focus, to keep her eyes open, but everything was just one big blur.

CHAPTER 17

CARTER STARED at the dot on his phone. Mia hadn't answered any of his calls and he'd gone from assuming she was on her way to the ranch to actively worrying that something had happened. He'd been pissed when he came home and she wasn't there. He'd tried to warn her going out wasn't a great idea but he hadn't wanted to scare her to death about her uncle and that her life might be in danger.

The dot wasn't moving and his mood shifted from pissed to worried. He grabbed his keys and raced from the cabin. Two minutes later, his tires squealed as he roared around a curve and raced down the road toward the stationary dot. If anything had happened to Mia, he wouldn't forgive himself.

Mia opened her eyes and couldn't understand where she was. It took a full minute for her to comprehend that she was on her left side looking out the splintered but still intact windshield. The headlights of her car lit up the trees and disappeared into the sky. She took a deep breath then halted abruptly as pain screamed through her torso. Breathing shallowly, she inventoried her state, raging headache and her mouth tasted coppery. Wiggling her fingers and toes for reassurance, she concluded that other than a bump on the head and some hopefully just bruised ribs, she was all right. *Thank God for the airbags.* The blood in her mouth was probably a result of the airbag inflating right in her face. Her lip stung when she ran her tongue over it, likely a cut also from the shock of the airbag. Still, she was alive.

Gravel crunched and footsteps scraped along, and she froze. Someone had run her off the road. Were they coming back to help, or finish the job? Someone was coming down the embankment. Two someone's by the sound of things.

Terror made her heart slam double-time, making her breathe even more shallowly. What the hell was she going to do? Even if she could get her seatbelt undone, she would have to crawl up across the passenger seat and go out the passenger side window and then she'd have to jump down to the ground. She wasn't sure she could do it.

The sounds were louder now. Mia swore. She didn't have a choice. Chances were good whoever it was would try and kill her. She couldn't stay there and help them succeed. She jabbed the release button on the seatbelt hard, and thankfully, it freed her. It took several tries to shift enough to get her feet beneath her, Finally, she crouched with her feet straddling the open space where the driver's side window used to be.

She tried to straighten up and pull herself upward, but she didn't have the strength in her arms and her ribs protested the harsh pulling of each attempt.

She glanced out the windshield. Maybe she could push it out and get out that way. She'd just lifted one foot to kick at it when a voice said, "Don't fucking move."

She jumped and let out a small scream. Looking up, she met the gaze of Mikey. He was looking down at her through the passenger-side window. "What do you want, Mikey? Why did you run me off the road?" she demanded.

He just grunted and she quickly concluded that he was having problems climbing onto the side of the car. While he was struggling with that, she could still kick out the windshield and get away. She gave it a kick, once, twice, and then pushed at it with her hands.

"What the fuck are you doing? Stop it. Stop or I'll shoot you."

Mia looked up at him again. He was still struggling to get onto the side of the car, gun clutched awkwardly in his hand. She had nothing to lose because he sure as hell wasn't planning to let her leave the car alive. Even with a massive headache, she knew he was going to shoot her either way.

She continued to push and the window gave way. She half stepped, half fell out of the car onto what remained of the windshield and the ground. Pushing herself to her feet, she turned to run and skidded to an abrupt halt. There in front of her was Nakoa, the gun in his hand aimed directly at her heart.

～

CARTER'S STOMACH was in knots as he broke every speed limit posted to get to the stationary dot. He rounded the last curve and swore. An SUV was parked haphazardly on the other side of the road. No headlights, and no movement from inside.

Carter slowed down as quickly as he could without locking up the brakes. He pulled over to his side of the road and turned off his truck. Then he hopped out, grabbing his gun from his waistband. He moved quietly to the other vehicle and peered through the gangster blacked-out windows. Empty.

The sound of voices floated up to him. Cautiously, he moved around to look over the side of the embankment. The scene below made his heart stop. Mia, lit up by the beams of her headlights, standing with her hands in the air.

"Nakoa, what the hell are you doing?" Mia cried.

"Shut up, Mia."

Carter strained but he couldn't make out the other man, Nakoa, in the darkness. He stood outside the glare of the headlight beam.

Another man approached Mia from behind.

"Don't stand there, you stupid fuck. I'll end

up shooting you," Nakoa yelled from the darkness.

"I was just trying—" the other man started.

"Get out of the fucking way," Nakoa snarled.

Carter wanted to shoot him, but he couldn't see him enough to be sure, and if he missed, then Nakoa would be free to shoot Mia. He aimed instead for the man behind Mia. He fired off a shot and the man screamed as he went down on one knee. Carter quickly moved from his position and started down the embankment keeping low so he wouldn't be framed against the night sky.

Nakoa fired off a shot toward where Carter had been and then fired another one in his general direction.

"Nakoa, help me. You gotta help me. I'm hit," the other man wailed.

"Shut up, Mikey."

"Come on, brother," he moaned.

Carter was almost down to the bottom of the embankment. He lost sight of Mia on his way down, but he was confident she'd gotten away.

Nakoa was still outside the beam of light so Carter couldn't get a fix on him. He waited, hoping Nakoa would come forward to help

Mikey. The sound of sirens ripped through the darkness.

Nakoa swore and lunged for Mikey. He grabbed the other man and pulled him out of the light. Carter could've shot him but with the cops arriving any minute, it might have been difficult to explain why he was shooting at a man who wasn't shooting at him. He moved forward and started searching for Mia. She couldn't have gotten far.

The sound of an engine reached him. Nakoa and Mikey were leaving. That was good and bad. "Mia," he yelled. "It's me. Where are you?"

"Carter?" her voice came from his right.

"Mia?"

"I'm here." came her response and then he saw movement.

The cops arrived and were shining their flashlights down the embankment, calling out to see if anyone responded. He made it to her in four long strides. "Mia," he said before promptly wrapping her in his arms.

"Thank God!" she mumbled into his chest.

Flashlight beams lit them up and then they were surrounded. The sound of an ambulance arriving above drowned out the officers' chatter.

Mia pulled away from Carter and put a hand

up to block the light. "I…I," she started and then her legs gave out. Carter caught her and immediately picked her up. He made his way back off the embankment with her in his arms. His pulse was pounding due to the exertion and his relief that he'd gotten to her in time. He set her down again by the ambulance.

"No, I don't need—"

"Let them check you over. It was a bad accident." He captured her gaze and tried to ask how she wanted to deal with this, but she seemed dazed. *Shit. Did she have a concussion?*

"Miss Ryan?" an officer asked.

Mia nodded.

"Okay," the officer said, "let the EMTs check you over and then we'll talk about your accident." He leaned toward her. "Have you been drinking?"

She bit her lip. "I had two sips of wine at Ohana's. Talk to Dahlia, the bartender. She can tell you how much she poured me and how little I drank. You can check my blood alcohol if you want. I'll be under the legal limit."

She glanced at Carter, and this time she gave him a look that said *keep your mouth shut*. He gave her a discreet nod to let her know her message was received. He didn't figure she'd want to tell the truth at this stage. It would just bring up everything else. Besides, if she didn't say anything, it meant that he might get another crack at hurting Donny. He wanted to take that bastard out for hurting Mia in the worst way.

"Let's get you checked and then we'll talk." The officer nodded to the EMTs and then turned to Carter. "And you are?" he said as he led Carter a few steps away from the ambulance.

"I'm Mia's boyfriend, Carter Nolan."

"Okay, Mr. Nolan. How did you come to be here?"

Carter glanced over at Mia. She was on a stretcher now and the EMT was looking at her ribs. "Mia was coming over to my place—"

"And where is that?" the officer asked.

Carter explained that he was staying on Hawk's ranch for a while doing equipment tests for the military."

The officer's demeanor immediately changed. "You're one of Hawk's boys? Okay then, what happened?" The cop seemed to relax instantly.

"Mia was on her way over and I thought it was taking too long, so I called her. When she didn't answer, I checked her location on my phone. I have her on an app." Guilt flashed through him. He hadn't told Mia that he had tagged her phone so he could locate her if he needed to. He was going to have to explain that one. It was standard protocol in a security scenario, but since they were sort of dating, did that make it stalkery?

"Can't be too careful these days," the officer said.

"When she didn't move for a bit, and didn't answer her phone, I came to see if she was okay. I had just found her when you guys arrived."

He had no problem lying to the cop. Whatever kept Mia safe. He wasn't sure if she thought going to the cops was a good idea or a bad one at this point. He had his own opinion on that score, but he needed to speak with her first.

"Okay. Thanks." The officer said and then headed over to the ambulance. Mia was sitting up now. "She okay?"

The EMT nodded. "Cut lip and some bruised ribs but other than that she's fine. A couple days of taking it easy and she'll be good as new."

"Miss Ryan, can you tell me what happened?"

Mia licked her lip and winced. She shot a quick look at Carter and then said, "I guess I must have dozed off. Been working long hours lately. Honestly, I don't know what happened."

"I see," the officer commented. "You weren't

talking to anyone on your phone or maybe sending a text?"

She shook her head. "No. Oh, my God. My purse. It's still in the car. My phone is in it." She looked beseechingly at Carter.

The officer keyed his radio and asked one of the other cops down by the car to check for the bag. Turning back to Mia, he said, "And you're sure there was nothing else? No one else involved?"

"No, just me. So sorry, Officer." Mia closed her eyes and then rubbed her face with her hands.

Carter took that as his cue. "Do you think maybe I could take her home?"

The cop turned to look at him just as another officer appeared with Mia's bag. She reached for it, but the officer offered it to the cop who was questioning her. "Do you mind?" he asked.

Mia shook her head.

The officer opened the bag. He dug around a bit and then pulled out her cell phone. He stowed the device back in the bag and returned it to Mia with a look at Carter. "You can take her home. Just drop by the station to file the report for your insurance," he said to Mia.

She nodded her thanks. Carter helped her

climb out of the ambulance. "You okay?" he asked in a quiet voice as he led her to his SUV.

"Not really. Thanks for saving my life. It was you, wasn't it? You shot Mikey?"

"Yeah." He opened the door of the SUV and helped Mia into the passenger seat.

He was guiding the seat belt around her body when she murmured, "This is the nightmare that keeps on giving."

Carter agreed wholeheartedly, and it was only going to get worse.

CHAPTER 18

MIA SWALLOWED the pain pills Carter had given her with her tea and then leaned back into the sofa cushions.

"Why don't you go get ready for bed?" Carter suggested.

"In a bit. I just need a moment to…."

Carter sat down next to her and put his hand on her thigh. "You scared the hell out of me."

"I scared me, too. When I looked over and saw nothing but air I thought I was done. God that noise when the car rolled, it was so loud and crazy. My poor car." That was an expense she hadn't planned on. Insurance would cover some, but it wasn't likely to buy her a brand new car. She'd have to go searching to find something she could afford.

"Mia, do you know why that guy wanted to kill you?"

She shook her head. "I've been trying to figure that the whole ride home. Nakoa and Mikey work for Bobby. They've always been nice to me in the past." She shook her head. "Why would Bobby suddenly think it was a good idea for me to be dead? Did he get his money another way? Am I just a loose end? If that's the case, then so are Akela and Kai." She stared at Carter. "Do you think I should call them, warn them?"

Carter rubbed the back of his neck. "God's honest truth? I have no idea. Do you think your uncle might be on to Bobby and again, Bobby is afraid that you'll tell your uncle that he's trying to take over the gambling ring?"

"That's a possibility, and probably the more likely scenario. If my uncle suspected Bobby was trying to oust him and set up his own gambling business again, and taking my uncle's clients, then he would be very pissed off. Bobby would want to reassure him that he wasn't doing that. Having me around could be a threat. I don't think he knows that Makaio is my uncle, but he probably knows we've met and that Uncle Makaio knows who I am." She rubbed her forehead. "Bobby knew how much money I made when I was gambling so he had to have someone on the inside. If that person told Bobby that Makaio came over and spoke to me, it might have spooked him. Maybe that's why he sent Nakoa and Mikey." She rubbed circles on her temples. All this thinking and assumption was making her headache worse.

Carter cocked his head. "It's a thought. Let's think about it some more in the morning. I, for one, am flat-out exhausted. It's been a long day and an even longer night." He leaned over and kissed Mia on the forehead. "You aged me tonight. The thought that Donny might hurt you just about did me in."

She offered him a small smile. "Thank you for saving my ass."

He grinned. "It's such a cute ass, I couldn't let anything happen to it." Mia yawned and Carter laughed. "Off to bed with you. You need some rest." He gently helped her up from the sofa and walked with her into the bedroom.

Mia couldn't wait to crawl into bed. She was beyond exhausted but more. She couldn't wait to have Carter's arms around her. Then and only then would she feel truly safe.

~

MIA SLIPPED SOUNDLESSLY out of Carter's arms and quickly gathered her things. She stepped into the bathroom and started the arduous task of getting dressed. Her ribs were on fire. She pulled on her clothing and then immediately searched the bathroom for some Advil. Finding some, she took two and then looked at herself in the mirror. A jagged dark line marred her swollen lip, and the skin under her eyes might be slightly bruised and, based on her cheeks feeling stung, she suspected she had a rash from the chemicals in the deploying airbag. Probably a good thing the light in the bathroom was dismal. The airbag had done a number on her, but it had saved her life so she couldn't complain.

Exhaustion made the fine lines around her eyes look deeper and the frown lines around her mouth more pronounced. She would love to crawl back into bed with Carter and stay there for the foreseeable future. That idea was bliss. Carter coming to help her after she'd managed to get out of the car last night was nothing short of miraculous and she would owe him forever.

But after he'd fallen into a much-deserved sleep, Mia had lain there staring at the ceiling. She was safe because Carter made her safe but at what cost? Her safety put him in danger. He'd risked his life to come find her and save her. Nakoa could have shot him. That was such a terrifying thought that even though she was in pain and beyond exhausted, she hadn't been able to sleep.

It was time to go to the cops. One cop specifically. She had to talk to Emery. By now her friend would have heard that Mia was gambling again. The question was, did she think it was because Mia was doing it for fun, or did she know anything about Bobby? Emery had sent her a couple of texts last night, but Mia hadn't responded. Once she got into work this morning, she'd no doubt hear about Mia's accident, and then she would have all kinds of questions.

Emery would also know Mia lied to the cops. Emery knew Mia well enough to know that she would never, under any circumstances, drive if she was that tired. After what happened with her parents, Mia had adhered to strict rules about driving safety.

Mia let out a long breath. The only thing to do was go see Emery. Maybe she could help Akela and Kai. Maybe there was something she could do about Bobby, too, although Mia had her doubts. Either way, Mia was just going to have to tell Emery what was going on and let the chips fall where they may. Because there was no way Emery was going to let any of this go.

More importantly or even if she were being totally honest, her involvement in Bobby's scheme would be exposed, and Carter would no longer be in danger from trying to protect her. She couldn't deal with that. The thought that he might get hurt because of her was just too much. She wouldn't let that happen.

Mia did her best to look at least halfway decent. Quietly, she slipped from the bathroom and sneaked out of the cabin. Like before, she called an Uber and met it by the gate. She didn't breathe a sigh of relief until they were halfway to town. She didn't want Carter to try and stop her. He still wasn't keen on her going to the cops until they knew more.

She turned and craned her neck to see behind her and then swore silently. Her ribs protested her movement, but at least there weren't any cars behind the Uber. She didn't think Bobby and his goons would try anything in broad daylight, but it didn't hurt to be vigilant.

Ten minutes later she got out of the rideshare at Emery's house. A van with the words *Tropical Landscapers* on the side of it blocked Emery's driveway. There was a guy hauling gardening stuff from the cargo space. Working two jobs must really pay well if Emery could afford a landscaper.

Mia went around the van, smiling a greeting to the guy, and started up the driveway. The house was a cute little place, just like Mia's. Perfect for one or maybe two people, she thought. Carter's face popped into her mind. She let out a sigh. No point in dwelling on that thought.

Mia glanced at her watch. Just after six a.m. Hopefully, Emery was drinking her first cup of coffee for the day, which would be good because Mia could sure use a cup herself. If not, Mia would wake her and make the coffee while she waited. A sound behind her made her turn just as the man from the van put something over her nose and mouth. She tried to fight, to scream but the smell was overpowering and made her woozy. She flailed but her limbs were just so heavy, like she'd strapped weights around them. Her eyelids closed. She sagged and her last thought was of Carter. At least he was safe.

CHAPTER 19

MIA'S RIBS hurt enough that it finally roused her. There was a bag over her head, which made it difficult, but not impossible, to see. The loose weave of the fabric allowed her limited vision. And she wasn't happy with what she could see.

She was in the back of a van but that's all she knew. It smelled like earth. It had to be the land-scape van that was blocking Emery's driveway. She'd tried moving and discovered that someone had tied her hands behind her back. Between the fiery tingles from her arms and, of course, her ribs, any movement stung. Her feet were tied as well, Pain radiated through her jaw as she tried to force the smelly gag from her mouth.

Mia fought to stay calm. Kidnapped was

better than dead. If Bobby wanted her dead as she suspected, then he could've gotten her in a drive-by shooting or even walked up to her and stabbed her. Instead, he had his goons grab her. That had to be a good thing, didn't it?

A good thing? God, panic made her think such inane things. She started to laugh, a high pitched hysterical laugh. Here she was thinking that being kidnapped was a good thing.

What the hell had happened to her life? Where had it taken such a wrong turn?

The van made a sharp turn, and she swore again as her right arm pressed against her ribs. The ground they were driving over was smooth-ish, so it was paved but it had the odd bump here and there. The sound of birds reached her ears as the van rolled to a stop. The clang of metal and engines was loud. She knew the sound, but she couldn't place it. Where was she?

A door slammed shut. Was someone coming to get her? She tried to come up with a plan to escape but her mind was blank. The van's rear doors opened, and light came through the weave of the bag. The smell hit her next. Salt?

Then all the pieces fell into place. They were on the docks. It had to be the Port of Hilo by the level of sound. Kawaihae was smaller and not as busy. The feeling of relief at knowing where they'd taken her died as suddenly as it arose. Were they going to put her into a container ship and send her out to die at sea? Mia did her best to not hyperventilate.

Unceremoniously, someone hauled her out of the van. Without a word, she was slung over a shoulder like a feed sack. Her ribs screamed with each jolt as the person carried her into what she assumed was a warehouse. The way the sound echoed, the place seemed to be large. The open weave of the bag over her head allowed her to glimpse pallets, but not enough to see what was on them. Her body crashed on the beefy shoulder with each step as he climbed a staircase. She heard voices and smelled machine oil. Did no one care that she was being carried over some rando guy's shoulder with her hands and feet tied and a bag over her head?

The guy paused and she heard the click of a door opening before he proceeded. The sound changed, became less echoey. Must be an office. She was dropped unexpectedly onto a hard surface, forcing out a muffled scream as pain from her ribs radiated through her entire torso. She was half-lying, half-sitting with her arms still behind her back. It was too difficult to sit upright with her legs still tied. She couldn't get any purchase to right herself. Someone pulled the bag off her head, and she blinked in the sudden light.

"Mia, I'm so glad you could join me today."

She turned her face toward the voice. Her uncle was sitting at a large desk with his hands steepled in front of him. "It's been far too long since we've spoken. We're family, we need to chat more often, don't you agree?" He gestured to his goon to remove the gag.

Gag free, Mia still said nothing. Her mouth was too dry to form a single word. She'd been thinking Bobby had been behind the attempt on her life but maybe her uncle was the culprit. But why would he want her dead? Did he really believe she ratted out his gambling establishment?

"It's rude not to speak when spoken to. I know your mother would have taught you that."

She still stayed silent. Honestly, she had no idea what to say.

"Tea?" he asked gesturing to the tea service beside him.

It was so insane that she wanted to laugh. *I just had you kidnapped but you look a little parched. Tea?* The cup and saucer were porcelain with a lovely rose pattern, so incongruent in the rough office.

She nodded. "Yes, I would love some tea." Her voice came out a little raw. She couldn't give a flying fig about tea, but it would mean she would get her hands unbound, and the cup and saucer were breakable, so maybe, just maybe, she could break them and get a shard of porcelain with a sharp edge to use as a weapon.

Her uncle poured her a cup and gestured toward the milk. She nodded. Then the goon, who was a large man of Samoan descent, cut the zip ties binding her hands. His black eyes were lifeless and terrifying, and Mia had no doubt that if her uncle gestured toward her, the man would snap her neck just as easily as he was handing her the cup and saucer.

She righted herself and took the tea, promptly resting it on her lap. Her hands were shaking which caused the cup to rattle against the saucer. Her uncle took a sip of his, with his pinky thrust into the air as though he was taking tea with Lili'uokalani, the overthrown queen of Hawai'i. Mia fought a hysterical laugh at the incongruity of the situation. Her uncle very deliberately placed the cup back on the saucer.

"I must say, Mia, you look so much like your

mother," his voice hardened as he continued, "which is too bad because I have always hated her. I'm trying not to hold it against you."

"Big of you," she blurted. Damn! She needed to keep her mouth shut, now of all times.

The door to the office opened and Donny strode in.

Mia blinked.

Was Donny working for her uncle? Did her uncle know that this man was working with Bobby to take over the business? Was this a possible bargaining chip? Hope rose that maybe she could get Donny to help her escape. Donny met her gaze and her stomach lurched. All thoughts of getting his help vanished. There was no way he would help her, not the way he looked at her. He was more likely to rape and then kill her.

"I see you found her in one piece," Donny commented. "Glad to see that the accident didn't wreck your face." His eyes traveled down her body. "Or any other part of you."

The nausea rose fast and hot, and she barely held back the vomit.

"Yes, I must say I was surprised that you, of all people, fell asleep while you were driving. I would have thought losing your parents in a car crash would have left a stronger impression on you." Her uncle sipped his tea.

Mia stared at him and frowned. Did he really think she fell asleep? How would he know? He must have an informant at the police department. But that made no sense, because if he did, why didn't they warn him about the raid?

"I didn't fall asleep. Someone ran me off the road." She didn't say anything else because she was too damn confused about what was going on. She took a page out of her uncle's book and sipped her tea. It felt good on her throat and slightly warmed her insides which had turned to ice.

"Why would someone run you off the road, Mia?"

"Uncle Makaio, I have no idea. Why don't you tell me?" she said with a lot more bravado than she felt.

"Me?" Her uncle raised his eyebrows. "Now why would I do that?"

"No clue. But you kidnapped me so there must be something you want from me. If it's not me dead, then what is it?"

Her uncle smiled "Oh, I just want to have a little chat with you. Then we'll see if your death will be necessary, shall we? After all, I wouldn't want to have to kill *all* my family."

Mia's heart stuttered to a stop as her blood ran cold. There was no doubt in her mind. Her uncle had just confessed to killing her parents and she was probably next.

CHAPTER 20

CARTER'S CELL RANG, waking him instantly. He grabbed his phone. "Nolan," he growled.

"Carter, man wake up," Flint's voice cut through the fog.

"What's wrong?" Carter demanded as he sat up and looked around. Where the hell was Mia? The bathroom door was open so he knew she wasn't in there. His heart thundered.

"It's Mia. She was kidnapped from Emery's."

Carter bounded to his feet and spun in a circle. "Did Emery see who took her? Did she call it into the PD?" He immediately got his go bag and threw it on the bed.

"Emery has the guy on video. She heard something and went to look. She said she missed it by maybe five minutes. That was about twelve minutes ago. She knows Mia's involved in something and she wants to talk to you before calling it in."

"Give her my number. I need five minutes." Carter cut the call and went into the bathroom. He took an ice-cold, three-minute shower, and then dressed in his gear. Black cargo pants and a black t-shirt. He was adding his weapons when his phone rang again.

"Emery," he barked, "tell me."

"Carter, I could fucking kick myself. I heard a sound and it took me a minute to drag my ass out of bed," Emery's voice sounded stressed.

"It's not on you. Give me the details."

Emery told him exactly what was on the video and then sent him the clip. "I found her purse on the sidewalk with her phone and everything in it. I'm just so fucking pissed at myself for not getting to her in time. Do you know who's behind this?"

Carter hesitated. "There are a few options."

"What? What the fuck has Mia gotten herself involved in?" Emery was pissed and Carter knew she was only going to get madder when he told her the rest.

"Look," he said as he slammed the door to his cabin. "I'm..." he glanced toward his truck. Flint,

Quinn, and Bowie were standing next to it, dressed in their gear ready to go. "We're on the way to you. I will explain everything once we get there."

"Fine. I'll be standing by," she said before clicking off the call.

Carter raced toward the truck. "This shit Mia's involved in, it's bigger than we thought. I—"

"Shut the fuck up and get in the vehicle," Bowie groused. "It's too fucking early to be out here and I haven't had enough coffee. You can tell us everything when we get there."

"I'm with Bowie," Quinn growled.

"Dude, did you really think we wouldn't come with you?" Flint snorted. "You're not *that* much of an idiot. Let's go. Emery has coffee on."

Carter just nodded and pulled open the driver's side door of the SUV. He knew his team; his brothers were with him, not even thinking about making him ask for their help. Their support warmed his icy heart.

IN NO TIME, he pulled into Emery's driveway. The four of them trooped into the house and

Emery handed each man a mug. She turned to Carter. "Start talking and it had better be fucking good."

Carter filled them in on what had been happening over the last couple of weeks.

Emery swore. "Stupid. Why the hell didn't she come to me?"

"Because she didn't want to put you in the position of having to choose between her and your job. She knows how much you love what you do. Mia didn't want the cops involved because she also knew that they'd keep her on the inside anyway because she was sure they'd want an inside person. Plus, there was Akela and her brother to think about."

Emery sighed. "She's not wrong. The DA would've kept her in, but they would've protected her. And yeah, there's not much I could have done about Akela."

Carter could point out that he'd been there to protect her but she'd still gone out on her own. He was pissed at her for doing it. Taking the risk the first time was bad enough but doing it a second time? What the hell had she been think-ing? He was determined to find her and ask her.

"They must have followed her from the ranch," Emery pointed out. "There's no way they were staking out my place just in case she came by."

"But how would they know she was there?" Quinn asked.

Emery snorted. "It's not like you guys have been subtle. You've all been hanging at Ohana's and," she turned to Carter, "you and Mia have been seen together. They didn't have to be geniuses to figure out where you would take her if things got crazy. They just had to ask around a bit."

Carter grunted in acknowledgment. Emery was not wrong. They probably had the road to the ranch staked out. He should've thought of that.

"This Bobby guy is who ran her off the road last night?" Flint asked.

"His goons. Nakoa and Mikey," Carter confirmed.

"Okay, we just have to find him," Bowie commented. "Emery, where would he hang out?"

Carter held up his hand. "There's more."

"What the fuck? How can there be more?" Emery slammed her mug down on the counter. "Jesus, it's only been a couple of weeks. What else could Mia be involved in?"

"Makaio Hale is involved," Carter announced.

Emery's eyes narrowed. "Involved how? I know Mia was gambling at his place to get the money but what does that have to do with anything."

"Makaio is her uncle."

Emery's breath hissed out. "Son of a bitch. That's one hell of a secret to keep."

"Who's Makaio Hale?" Flint asked.

"He's one of the biggest organized crime bosses in the whole state. He usually stays in Oahu, but he's been on the island for the last couple of weeks. Rumor has it he's making some kind of real estate deal, but no one knows too much about it."

Carter didn't care. He just wanted to find Mia. Standing here talking had been killing him, while she was out there somewhere, in God only knew what kind of condition. But he also knew the best way to find her was to have a plan and that's what they needed to do now."

"You're saying this crime boss might want to kidnap her as well? It could be either of them?" Quinn asked.

Carter nodded. "Makaio might think it was Mia who dropped the dime on his gambling den. Mia was invited to be there and we were on the way when we saw all the cop cars. We didn't stick around nor did we say anything. Makaio might hold a grudge."

Emery snorted. "That's for fucking sure. If he thinks Mia ratted out his operation, then he would have to make an example out of her. He can't have people screwing up his business without getting punished."

Carter's already knotted gut spasmed. He needed to get out there. He needed to find Mia before... well he just couldn't go down that road.

"Emery, can you get a list of places that Makaio and Bobby might take her? We'll divide and conquer. Whoever finds a likely spot, we'll regroup there and form a plan." Carter looked at his teammates, who all nodded.

"Okay, that makes sense," Bowie nodded. "Let's do teams of two though. We don't want to be spread too thin. It's unfamiliar territory and we don't know who all the players are."

Carter wanted to argue. They needed to cover as much ground as possible, but Bowie had a point. They had to be smart about this. Mia being kidnapped was killing him. His heart hurt and his thinking was foggy. He needed to get his shit together if he was going to be able to help her at all. "Two-man teams," he agreed. "Emery, give us a place to start and then feed us more locations as you get them." He turned to Quinn. "You're with me."

Quinn nodded.

"Be safe," Emery said as the guys headed out the door. She was already working the phone for information as they walked out.

Carter walked toward the SUV. His body was tied up in knots and icy fingers gripped his heart. *Please, God, don't let us be too late.*

CHAPTER 21

"YOU KILLED MY PARENTS?" Mia wanted it to come out as a scream, but her voice was barely above a whisper.

Her uncle smiled icily. "Yes, and do you know why?"

She could only stare. All this time she'd thought it was Bobby. That wasn't exactly true. She'd half-thought it was Bobby. The other half of her believed the cops when they said it was an accident. And all this time, her own uncle was responsible for killing her parents.

"Because of what your mother did?"

"What the hell could she have done that was so bad?" Mia demanded. "She was your sister. Your own flesh and blood."

Makaio slammed his hand on the desk,

rattling the tea set. "Yes, she was, and I hated her. She was always the favorite. Always got everything she wanted. Always had our father's favor. But I could live with all that. I would have happily gone on ignoring her. But she crossed the line. She interfered in my world and for that she had to die."

"I don't understand. How did she interfere in your world? She avoided you just like you avoided her."

Her uncle poured himself more tea as if he discussed murdering his family members every day. But Mia caught the tremor in his hand and the flush on his cheeks. He was seriously angry. It made Mia's throat close, and she struggled to pull in a deep breath.

"She did right up until her daughter started to gamble and then she stepped over the line." Makaio met her gaze with his own frigid stare.

"I don't know what you're talking about. She and Dad staged an intervention, and I stopped gambling. What did that have to do with you?"

Her uncle snorted. "An intervention, ha. I guess she wasn't so sure it would work, or she just didn't trust your word. Your mother ratted out Bobby Kamaka's gambling ring. *She* told the cops where to find him."

Mia was confused about so many things. "But I thought Bobby didn't work for you then."

"I didn't know about his gambling ring at that point. He managed that on his own," her uncle agreed. "But he was running drugs for me and when your mother gave the location of the next game to the police, it happened to be when Bobby was moving a large shipment of drugs for me. They were confiscated and I had to pay the owner of those drugs for the loss of them and another fee on top of that just to keep him happy. I don't like having to pay out and not make anything back. That was on your mother. What kind of a businessman would I be if I let the people who caused me problems get away with it?"

Mia wanted to hurl the cup and saucer at her uncle. The teacup dipped dangerously in her fingers thanks to her sweaty palms. "But you waited a long time to get your revenge."

"I wanted to make sure if there were any issues that Bobby would be able to take the blame. Fortunately, there were none. It went smoothly."

"I hate you," Mia blurted. "I hate you so fucking much I want to kill you."

"I'm sure you do but you're not going to get

that chance because we're here now to determine you told the police about Peter and the gaming room at the warehouse. If it was, then you will suffer the same fate as your parents, only yours will be so much more painful."

The door opened and Donny walked in, followed by the man who'd been at the warehouse when her uncle first walked. What had Carter called him? Bascom. Carter had said Bascom was a powerful man with lots of connections in Washington. She didn't want to know what he had to do with her uncle.

"They're here. It's time," Bascom announced.

Her uncle stood up. "We'll continue this later, Mia. Have a good long think on what we've spoken about." He gestured toward the goon who had been standing in the corner of the room waiting on her uncle's next command. He came toward her.

"Donny," her uncle added as he turned toward the other man, "go find Bobby. I want to speak with him later."

Donny left the room, followed by Bascom and her uncle.

The man who'd kidnapped her took the teacup from her and set it on the desk. Then he stood her up, zip-tied her hands behind her back again, and put the bag back over her head. He pushed her down on the sofa where she fell over onto her side. She swore silently as pain flared from her ribs.

At least he hadn't put the gag back in her mouth. *Be thankful for small mercies* her mother would always tell her. *It's hard to be thankful at the moment, Mom.* Tears clogged her throat as she thought of her parents. She swallowed hard and then pushed those thoughts away. She didn't have time for that now. She needed a plan to get out of this mess and it had better be good because things weren't looking so great for her, and she was determined to make sure her uncle didn't get away with murdering her as well as her parents.

MIA OPENED HER EYES. The bag was still over her head, but the office was dark now. She'd spent the day on the couch with her hands and everything hurt. Her arms were numb. The man who'd kidnapped her had taken her to the restroom twice, and she'd been allowed to have some more tea, but that was it.

She raised her head and waited a beat, but no

one yelled or said anything. Maybe they'd left her alone. It wasn't like she could go anywhere. Or so they thought. Mia had other ideas. She swung her legs down off the couch and tried to push herself into a sitting position. It was much easier now that her feet weren't tied together. The trips to the restroom had taken care of that. The goon had re-fastened her hands but not her feet. She still sent a silent thanks to Emery and Dahlia for making her workout. Those core muscles really came in handy.

Taking a deep breath, she tried to slow her heart rate to a normal rhythm. "Okay, you can do this," she murmured to herself. She strained to see through the bag but the darkness in the office made it impossible. Closing her eyes, she pictured the layout of the office. Thanks to the conversation with her uncle earlier and her trips to the restroom, she was pretty sure she knew where everything was. All she had to do was get on her feet and move to the desk. *Sure. Easy peasy.* Then she just had to push the cup and saucer off the desk. *Not a problem.* But after that it got tricky. *Or maybe downright insane.* How the hell was she going to be able to get down to the floor and pick up a piece of the china to cut the zip ties? Yeah, that part of her plan needed work.

The sound of footfalls on the stairs sent her heart racing. *Too soon.* She needed to escape before her uncle came back. She'd tried to come up with a plan all day until exhaustion overtook her and she fell asleep. Now she was kicking herself for sleeping. *How could I be so stupid?*

The door opened and the lights came on. Mia tensed, waiting for her uncle to tell her it was time to die.

"We're alone at last," Donny said as he walked over and ran a hand down her arm. She tried to shy away from him, but it was hard with her hands still tied. None too gently, he jerked the bag off her head, and she blinked in the sudden light. Donny ran a hand down her cheek, and she willed herself not to vomit at the touch of his blunt fingertips.

Donny took a couple of steps back and leaned on the desk facing her. Sweat glistened on his forehead and he huffed and puffed after climbing the stairs. His girth had grown since she first met him. The fluorescent lighting wasn't kind to him, showing his wrinkles and jowls in all their glory. He looked closer to her uncle's age than Bobby's. Revulsion filled her and she had to swallow to stop the vomit from coming up this time.

Donny held on to the edge of the desk. "You

and I need to have a chat. I can help you, you know. Your uncle listens to me."

She couldn't help it, she burst out laughing at his oversized ego. "You're joking, right? You're nothing more than a henchman, an errand boy. My uncle does not listen to the likes of you." Mia knew she should keep her mouth shut but she was tired and scared and tired of being scared. What did she have to lose?

"You listen to me," Donny snarled as he took a step toward her.

Just then, the office door opened again, and her uncle walked in with his ever-present body-guard. He looked back and forth between Mia and Donny with narrowed eyes. "What's going on here?" he demanded as he crossed the room and took his seat behind the desk.

"Mia and I were just having a little chat, weren't we, dear." Donny's voice went smooth again and he offered her a smug smile.

Makaio glanced at Donny but let it go. "Mia, have you thought about what I said? I need you to tell me the truth or you won't like the conse-quences."

Mia shrugged. "Does it matter what I say? If I say yes, then you will kill me. And if I say no, you're still going to kill me, so why say anything at all?"

Her uncle leaned across the desk. "But Mia, dear, it's the *way* I kill you that's important. If you tell me the truth, I'll make it quick. If you lie to me or you don't say anything then I'll have to make it slow and oh so painful."

Her veins turned to ice. He meant it. Her uncle was a horrible man but he wasn't lying to her. She tried to swallow, but terror had closed her throat and she ended up coughing.

Makaio folded his hands in front of him on the desk. "Time to tell me the truth. Did you tell the police about my gambling hall?"

She stared at him. There was no point in lying but was there a point in delaying things? She'd been thinking about their conversation all day like her uncle had suggested and she'd come to some realizations, but she needed a few more pieces of the puzzle. "Um, what was my end game?"

Her uncle frowned. "What? What are you talking about?"

"Why would I tell the police about your gambling ring? How does that help me?" Maybe if she could draw things out a bit, a solution might present itself. At the very least she'd get the answers she wanted.

Makaio narrowed his eyes at her again. "You're stalling."

"Maybe." She lifted her shoulders awkwardly. "But it's a legitimate question. Why would I rat out the gambling hall?"

"Because you wanted to get back at your uncle," Donny supplied.

She turned toward him and curled up her lip. "But, dumbass," she snarled, "that only gets my uncle in trouble if they can prove it was his place which I'm quite sure they can't. And it doesn't solve my Bobby problem. Bobby said if I don't make money for him, he'll kill Akela and Kai. I do not want their deaths on my conscience so why would I stop the only avenue I have for making a ton of money?" She didn't mention that Bobby was planning to use the money to take over the gambling ring. That was the one bargaining chip she had left, and she didn't want to use it until absolutely necessary. She needed all the help she could get.

CHAPTER 22

"Looks like seven men from here," Carter said as he looked through the night vision scope. "What do you see, Quinn?"

"I count nine," came the response threw his earbud.

Carter swore. How could he have missed two?

"You didn't miss them. You can't see them from your angle," Quinn stated as if he could read Carter's mind. It had taken them all day to determine where Mia was being held. Turns out they call it the Big Island for a reason. It didn't help that her uncle had his fingers in a lot of pies, forcing them to have to check a lot of locations. Carter was on edge due to the amount of wasted time. He was starting to lose his shit and he knew it. The thought of Mia being held captive all day all but destroyed his concentration. He refused to believe she could be dead. That was an outcome he wouldn't recover from, for all kinds of reasons. The main one was that he was falling in love with her, and if he couldn't protect the people he loved, then what the hell was he doing?

A hand touched him on the shoulder. "We'll get her out," Flint said. "Just hang in there a little longer."

Carter nodded in the darkness. He'd given up any pretense at hiding how wrecked he was feeling hours ago. "I know," he commented as he turned. They walked back to the others just as Quinn arrived.

They'd taken up a position on the roof of a warehouse, kitty-corner from the warehouse where Makaio was holding Mia. At least, they'd assumed it was her uncle. Bobby had gone underground, and rumor had it he was in hiding, so chances were good he didn't have Mia.

Her uncle, on the other hand, had been seen out and about with Mark Bascom today and holding meetings with some developers. According to Emery's sources, Makaio wanted to build some kind of high-security resort for the ultra-wealthy here on the Big Island. Sounded like some kind of dark money gathering place to Carter. The US is a major tax haven for non-Americans. A place like Makaio wanted to build would attract dubious high rollers from around the world.

"You sure he's in there?" Flint said into the phone. He met Carter's gaze and gave him a nod. "Okay, thanks. Let me know when you're here." He hung up. "Emery says they saw Mia's uncle walk into the building a short time ago."

Bowie leaned against the stairwell door. "What's the plan?"

Carter blew out a long breath. "I wish we had the blueprints so we had a better idea of what we're up against."

"It would be better, but we've been in tougher situations than this and did just fine," Bowie reminded him.

Carter's thoughts instantly returned to the last few missions and how close they'd come to dying. He hoped Castle was making progress because now he had something he really wanted to live for.

Flint said. "I think this is how we proceed; Bowie and Carter go in. Quinn and I handle the outside. We'll call Emery when we're good."

"Flint, does she know we're keeping her and the cops a step or two behind?" Quinn asked.

Carter winced. "I'm sorry, Flint but I just don't want to screw this up. If they roll too soon, it could all go to hell and Mia could get hurt."

"I get it and I agree," Flint said. "Emery doesn't know and if we execute well, she won't know. So let's get this right, okay?" His phone went off. "It's Emery," he said and then answered. "Yeah." There was silence and then, "Do we know who?"

Carter's heart slammed against his ribcage fearing Emery was telling them Mia was dead. The last fucking thing in the world he wanted to hear.

"Okay, I'll let them know." He hung up again. "Emery says two of Makaio's men just drove a guy into the warehouse. He had a bag over his head. They're not sure who it is."

"Shit," Carter breathed. "This is going south fast."

"Agreed. Emery and her people are getting antsy. They only agreed to work with us because Emery asked and because Hawk spoke with his connections. We got to get moving if we're going to do this and keep it controlled."

Bowie smiled. "Let's go have some fun."

"I THOUGHT about what you said, Mia, and I found I couldn't argue with your logic, so I thought it was better to get it from the horse's mouth so to speak." Makaio gestured toward the door as two of his goons walked in with another man between them. A bag covered his head as well, but Mia knew right away it was Bobby. Her mouth went dry. What would he say? Was he going to make it worse for her? Was that even possible?

One of the men pulled the bag off and Bobby squinted and swore as he blinked in the light. His hands were tied behind his back, but his legs were free.

"Bobby, thanks for joining us." Her uncle gestured to the couch. The guy who had kidnapped Mia pushed Bobby down beside her.

Bobby glanced at her and he blanched. She looked over at Donny in time to see a look of terror cross his face before he schooled his features into a blank stare. *What the hell was going on?* Her heart raced. Mia decided she had nothing to lose. "I thought Bobby worked for you."

"He does," her uncle said. "But rumors have

been flying. Bobby seems overly ambitious these days." He turned to Bobby. "My niece tells me she didn't tell the police about my little gambling establishment."

"Niece?" Bobby blurted and then turned to stare at Mia.

Mia gave him a little shrug. He was obviously shocked. What he didn't know about her could fill an ocean. *Moron.*

"Yes," her uncle continued. "She says she had nothing to gain from it because you were making her gamble to make money for you. She says you threatened her friends."

Bobby swallowed convulsively. "I... I... She..." He looked at Mia again and then it was like a light bulb went on over his head. "She found out about the money laundering at Lono's. I was just keeping her in line. I didn't want her to go to the cops, so I threatened to kill her friends and blame her for the cooked books."

Oh my God. Mia closed her eyes briefly and swore a blue streak in her head. Served her right. She'd asked how this could be any worse.

Makaio steepled his fingers under his chin. "I see. And the money?"

Bobby shrugged. "I saw a way to make some money and keep her in line at the same time."

Mia couldn't believe what she was hearing. Did that mean that her uncle didn't know about the small games Bobby held in Akela's basement? No, he had to know about those but likely didn't know Bobby was skimming the profits. Was he aware that Bobby was plotting against him? Maybe.

Another thing had been bugging her all day. Her uncle seemed to believe the story she'd told the cops about falling asleep at the wheel. Was Bobby the source of that info? Why did he want her dead? He obviously didn't know she was his boss's niece, so why take out his cash source?

"Mia?" her uncle barked.

She started. "I'm sorry... What?"

"Are we boring you?" he demanded.

"No, I just..." she met Donny's gaze, and suddenly everything fell into place. Her blood roared in her ears and bile rose up her throat. "It was you," she blurted out. "You tried to kill me last night. You used Bobby's guys to run me off the road."

Makiao frowned and Bobby stared at her. "What are you talking about?"

"Nakoa and Mikey ran me off the road and tried to kill me last night. If Carter hadn't come along, I'd be dead." She turned back to Donny.

"This is all your doing." She seethed. This slimy bastard had tried to kill her. She'd love to return the favor. *Asshole.*

Donny held up his hands and his eyebrows went up. "I have no idea what you're talking about. Why would I want you dead?"

"Yes, Mia, do tell." Her uncle swung his chair around so he could see Donny who had been standing to his left by his desk. One of Makiao's men moved across the room and stood behind Donny, pushing him so he was now in front of the desk to the right of Mia.

"I—" he stared at the bodyguard. Then turned back. "I have no idea what you're talking about."

Bobby cocked his head. "That's how these guys found me. You ratted me out, you fucker." He tried to stand but the security guy beside him shoved him back down.

Mia locked eyes with her uncle. Heart hammering like she'd been holding her breath under a massive wave, she spoke. "Donny ratted out your gambling warehouse. He did it because he and Bobby were trying to take over your gambling business. But something between them must have changed. Maybe you offered him another job or more money or a bigger piece of the pie or whatever, and he changed his mind."

Donny's face flushed. "That's a bullshit story."

Makaio tapped his fingers on the desk and eyed the man. "I asked Donny to oversee some more of my...endeavors, keep an eye on my money."

Mia knew she had to continue now that she had her uncle's attention. She licked her lips. "Donny had a better offer. He couldn't tell Bobby he'd switched sides. Bobby would kill him. But if he told the cops about the warehouse then it would close down, and I couldn't gamble, so Bobby had no way to raise the cash. Donny would keep his relationship with both of you and he would be safe.

"The one sticking point of course is me. Donny needed a scapegoat to blame the whole warehouse debacle on. Someone had to be the snitch. If he blamed me then everyone would want me dead. But there was still the risk that I could convince you that I wasn't behind the raid. The best thing for Donny would be if I turned up dead and then no one would have a chance to question me. So, he got Nakoa and Mikey to run me off the road."

"I don't know what you're talking about," Donny fumed. His face was a dull red and sweat had broken out on his brow.

"She's right," Bobby admitted. "You were the one who told me that Mia called the cops. I believed you. You were so convincing." He turned to Makaio. "She's right. It was Donny. Donny did it all!"

Her uncle stood and Mia's stomach plummeted. Did he believe her? Would it make a difference even if he did, or was she dead anyway? She was about to stand up when she got a sudden whiff of smoke. Was something on fire?

Makaio growled, "Are you telling me Donny wanted to take the gambling business from me?" He glared at Bobby.

"You stole it from me first!" Bobby pointed out. "I just wanted it back. I was trying to raise the money to give you a down payment on it. Then I was going to give you a good deal. I want to run it, but I'll split the take with you."

"And the games you do run for me in basements all over the island, you were just skimming on those to pay me?"

"Yes!" Bobby agreed. He struggled to his feet.

"You were going to pay me with my own money?" Makaio thundered.

Bobby immediately realized his mistake. "No! I mean I—"

"That's exactly what he was going to do," Donny interjected, his smug smile back in place.

"Was he now? And what were you going to do? Rob me once you were overseeing more of my business?" Makaio pointed at him. "You were in on it with him." He nodded to his enforcer but Donny was faster. He pulled out a gun and aimed it at Mia's uncle. Suddenly, the lights went out, and the whole warehouse was plunged into darkness.

A gun went off and then another shot was fired from across the room. The door opened and Mia felt someone brush past her. Then running feet echoed around her. A sudden scream and more scuffling. The smell of smoke was undeniable now. The sound of crackling flames filled the air. As if on cue, an alarm blared, like anyone needed to hear that to know the warehouse was on fire.

Mia stood and glanced around the room. Her uncle's goon was on the floor, his eyes staring sightlessly as red soaked his chest. Trying not to panic or gag, she went to the doorway and looked down. The entire warehouse was on fire. Gunshots cracked occasionally and it sounded like there were multiple shooters. Mia coughed.

If she didn't do something soon, she would die here.

She started down the stairs keeping low and trying to breathe shallowly. It was hard to see, and the smoke made her eyes water. Not to mention her hands were still bound, throwing off her balance. She was halfway down the stairs when she tripped over something. Throwing herself against the railing, she righted herself and ignored the pain in her ribs. She looked down to find the man who'd kidnapped her was half-laying, half-hanging off the stairs. He was dead. That must have been the scream she'd heard.

She stepped over the man and continued down, finally reaching the bottom. The smoke was getting thicker, and she was having problems seeing where the door was. A figure came out of the smoke toward her. Donny raised his gun and pointed it at Mia. She opened her mouth to scream when a shot split the air, and red bloomed on the center of Donny's chest. He crashed to the floor in front of her. Mia looked up and almost fainted.

CHAPTER 23

CARTER CAUGHT Mia as she stumbled toward him. "Mia, honey, are you okay?"

"I am now," she croaked and rested her head on his chest.

His heart had stopped beating when he saw the man with a gun aimed at the woman he'd fallen in love with. If he'd been thirty seconds later, he'd have lost her. He pulled her to him and gave her a quick hug. He couldn't think about any of that now. He needed to get her out of there. "We have to get out of here. The whole place is going to go up."

She coughed again but nodded.

He pulled out a blade and cut the black plastic restraints on her wrists. "Hold on to my belt and I'll lead you out, okay?"

She nodded but coughed some more.

"Stay low. It will help with the smoke.

"Okay," she said. Her eyes were watering, and she started coughing again.

Carter turned, bent over, and waited for Mia to grab his belt. When he felt the tug of her hand, he started forward. Flames flared up every wall. Only the center part was clear since there were no pallets stacked there.

Carter led Mia down the center of the warehouse toward the door. A stack of pallets on their left gave way and fell in front of them. Carter swore but moved to his left and made it around them. The door was not far ahead, but pallets on the floor in flames were blocking it. They were going to have to go around them on the right.

Carter got them close to the obstacle and turned to tell Mia what they were going to do when he saw movement out of the corner of his eye. He turned back only to catch a two-by-four to the arm, knocking his gun out of his hand. Mia's uncle swung the board again and Carter had to jump to the side, pulling Mia with him. The board narrowly missed her, but she let go of his belt.

Carter pulled out another gun but lost

Makaio in the smoke. He looked around but didn't see Makaio. He turned to get Mia when the kingpin came out of the smoke again, two-by-four raised above his head. Carter raised his gun, but Mia was faster. She came out of the smoke and hit her uncle dead center of his chest with a burning hunk of wood. Her uncle dropped to his knees as an explosion rocked the warehouse. A stack of pallets started to fall. Makaio looked at the falling pallets and screamed.

Carter grabbed Mia's hand and ran as fast as he could through the smoke to the doorway. They didn't stop running until they reached the fire engines outside.

"STOP STARING AT ME," Mia rasped. "I'm fine."

God, he'd almost lost her. It was a miracle she was sitting on the floor of the ambulance in one piece. He was slowly starting to process that Mia was okay. All he wanted to do was pull her into his arms and never let her go. "Put the oxygen mask back on," he growled as he tried to rein in his emotions.

"Mia," Emery said as she came over and gave

her friend a long hug. "I was so worried about you."

"Me too," Mia said.

"Girl, you ever hold out on me like that again and I will kick your ass from here to next week. You understand me?" Emery demanded.

"Understood," Mia responded in a solemn voice.

"Good." Emery gave her another huge hug. "My people are going to want to talk to you about all this, but it can wait until the morning." She turned to Carter. "You take care of her."

"Will do." And he would, no matter what it took.

"Glad to see you're in one piece, Mia," Flint commented. He turned to Emery. "Did we get everyone?"

She nodded and pointed over towards a group of police cars. There were ten men in handcuffs. "All of Makaio's henchmen and Bobby."

Bowie and Quinn joined them at the back of the ambulance. "What about Mia's uncle?" Bowie asked.

Emery shook her head. "We didn't see him."

"He's dead," Carter supplied and then squeezed Mia's arm. He knew there was no love lost between them but still, he was Mia's family. "He tried to take us out on the way out the door, but Mia decked him and then a stack of burning pallets collapsed on him."

"I'm sorry, Mia," Bowie offered.

She shook her head and removed the oxygen mask from her face. "It's not a loss to me. He killed my parents."

Carter stared at her. "Are you sure?"

She nodded. "He confessed it to me earlier today. My mom called the cops on him back when I was gambling, and he lost his gambling ring. He wanted revenge for it."

Carter put an arm around her. He couldn't take not touching her any longer. She leaned into him, and sweet relief swept through him..

Emery grabbed Mia's arm. "I'm so sorry, Mia. You told me you thought your parents' deaths weren't an accident. I didn't listen."

Mia shrugged. "There was no proof. It's fine. My uncle got his punishment." She took a pull from the oxygen mask. "And so did Donny. He was about to shoot me when Carter got him first."

Emery glanced at Carter, and he confirmed it.

Flint crossed his arms over his chest. "So it looks like our work here is done." He winked at

Emery who just shook her head at him. But a soft smile played on her lips.

"You all can go home but we'll need statements. I want to see you all down at the station tomorrow. Agreed?"

"Agreed," Flint responded. Quinn and Bowie nodded.

Mia nodded as she closed her eyes.

"I'm going to take her back to her place. We'll be there in the morning," Carter agreed.

Mia straightened up and let the blanket that had been around her shoulders fall away. She put the oxygen mask down and stood up. Carter swooped down and picked her up. "You're tired and hurt. I've got you," was all he said, and she nodded. But the truth was, he just needed to hold her close to his heart.

CHAPTER 24

"PADDLE, PADDLE, PADDLE," Mia yelled as the wave rose behind them.

Carter paddled like he was being chased by a terrorist and caught the wave. He stood up on the board and rode the curl a short distance before falling off again.

Mia grinned. He was getting the hang of it. More importantly, he was enjoying it. The smile that lit his face as he paddled back out to her was all the payment she'd ever need.

"That was much better," she called when he got closer.

"I can see why you love to surf. It's kind of like flying. It's an amazing feeling." Carter sat up on his board as he drew up alongside her.

"Yes, it is. I don't do it nearly enough

anymore." Mia looked out at the waves. If this adventure taught her nothing else, it was that she needed to spend more time enjoying life and less time working.

"Did Emery say anything about what's going to happen to Akela and Kai?"

Mia nodded. "Akela has agreed to give evidence against Bobby. Emery said she and Kai should be fine. She thought the Assistant District Attorney in charge of the case probably wasn't going to prosecute Akela. She still has no money and has to rebuild her business but at least she won't be in jail." She smiled at Carter. "I still have the money I won. I thought I might give some to her, help her get back on her feet."

"I think that's an amazing thing to do. You're a generous woman," Carter commented but his face clouded over.

Icy fingers gripped Mia's chest. "What is it? What's wrong?"

Carter met her gaze. "Look Mia, I'm not sure what's going to happen. There are...things going on back on the mainland, work things, and I don't know how they're going to play out. I'm not sure how much longer I'll be here on the Big Island but if you're up for it, I would like to spend whatever time I have here with you. I've really come to love it here and you're a big part of that. When, or if, I have to leave, if you want to...let what's between us go, then I'll understand. My job... My life is just in flux at the moment so I can't make any promises."

She breathed a sigh of relief and then her heart fluttered in her chest. "Carter, I would be majorly pissed at you if we didn't spend all of the time you have left on the island together. I think you're amazing too." She smiled at him and willed the heat in her cheeks to disappear. "It's been a long time since something this great has come into my life and you're just blowing me away. I'm in this for the long haul, no matter where you end up. If you're game." *Please say yes. Please say yes.* She just couldn't imagine not seeing where their relationship was going.

Carter leaned over and kissed her. "That sounds like the best idea ever. I think we should celebrate, and I have some ideas on how we should do it."

"Oh yeah?" she breathed as the butterflies in her stomach took flight. She kissed him and then said, "Race you to shore," she called and turned her board toward the beach.

Team Koa Bravo
Bowie's Battle - Jen Talty
Carter's Battle - Lori Matthews
Flint's Battle - Kris Norris
Quinn's Battle - Regan Black

FREE WITH NEWSLETTER SIGN UP

FALLING FOR THE WITNESS

Risk Assessment

Visit <u>Https://www.lorimatthewsbooks.com</u> for details on how to purchase these novels or sign up for my newsletter.

ABOUT LORI MATTHEWS

Lori Matthews grew up in a house filled with books and readers. She was introduced to different genres because of her parents' habit of leaving books all over the house. Her mother read romance, and her father read thrillers. Her love of reading and books led to her becoming a librarian. She started her career as a public librarian and then eventually made her way into schools as a high school librarian with a stop in the corporate world along the way.

When her children went off to school, she finally had the time to pursue her first love, writing and she's been pounding the keyboard ever since. She's won numerous writing awards including two Daphne Du Maurier awards. She currently lives in New Jersey with her husband, two children, her crazy dog, and her grumpy cat.

Follow me on social media and be sure to visit my webpage to keep up on my news. https://lorimatthewsbooks.com

Facebook: https://www.facebook.com/Lori MatthewsBooks

X: https://www.x.com/_LoriMatthews_

Instagram: https://www.instagram.com/lori matthewsbooks/

Goodreads: https://www.goodreads.com/ author/show/7733959.Lori_Matthews

BookBub: https://www.bookbub.com/ profile/lori-matthews

BROTHERHOOD PROTECTORS

ORIGINAL SERIES BY ELLE JAMES

Remy (#1)

Gerard (#2)

Lucas (#3)

Beau (#4)

Rafael (#5)

Valentin (#6)

Landry (#7)

Simon (#8)

Maurice (#9)

Jacques (#10)

Brotherhood Protectors Yellowstone

Saving Kyla (#1)

Saving Chelsea (#2)

Saving Amanda (#3)

Saving Liliana (#4)

Saving Breely (#5)

Saving Savvie (#6)

Saving Jenna (#7)

Saving Peyton (#8)

Saving Londyn (#9)

Brotherhood Protectors Colorado

SEAL Salvation (#1)

Brotherhood Protectors

ABOUT ELLE JAMES

ELLE JAMES also writing as MYLA JACKSON is a *New York Times* and *USA Today* Bestselling author of books including cowboys, intrigues and paranormal adventures that keep her readers on the edges of their seats. When she's not at her computer, she's traveling, snow skiing, boating, or riding her ATV, dreaming up new stories. Learn more about Elle James at www.elle-james.com

Website | Facebook | Twitter | GoodReads |
Newsletter | BookBub | Amazon

Or visit her alter ego Myla Jackson at
mylajackson.com
Website | Facebook | Twitter | Newsletter

Follow Me!
www.ellejames.com
ellejamesauthor@gmail.com

f X ⊙

Made in the USA
Monee, IL
26 October 2024